STRUNG

PER JACOBSEN

STRUNG

STRUNG

Per Jacobsen

Copyright © 2021

Per Jacobsen & HumbleBooks

1st edition, 2021

Cover design: Per Jacobsen

ISBN: 978-87-973294-3-6

For Adrian & Sofia Jacobsen,
the two greatest gifts this life has given me.

ACT 1

EAST ALIN

"There's a bullet in my barrel,
but I don't know who it's for.
Through the windows to your soul
it's not you I see no more."
— *O. E. Geralt, In Other Words.*

— 1 —

Randall Morgan's first thought was that it had to be a joke. A prank, probably made in connection with Halloween, that was equally as distasteful as it was well-executed.

However, this thought was little more than a desperate defense mechanism, as Randall deep down was well aware that Halloween had long since passed. Besides, he didn't need to spend much time studying the details of the bizarre sight that the car's headlights had brought into focus on the other side of the rain-soaked windshield to know that it couldn't be a joke.

And should there, despite these things, still be a flicker of doubt in Randall's mind, it disappeared, when the autumn wind outside of the vehicle grew stronger for a moment and thus turned the lifeless man who was dangling from the lamppost around, so his face came into view.

His purple, swollen face.

You need to call the police.

Despite this thought, Randall remained seated with both hands clasped to the steering wheel, making no effort to move.

What are you waiting for? The phone is right there. You don't even have to lean over to grab it. So, pull yourself together and call the police!

He glanced over at the passenger seat. There was, as his inner voice had already concluded, no more than two feet's distance between his hand on the steering wheel and the telephone on the seat. And no, he wouldn't even have to lean over to reach it. Nevertheless, it felt like an insurmountable task.

For a long time, he sat like that, frozen with his hands glued to the rugged plastic surface of the wheel, unable to move. A couple of times, his gaze wandered back to the hanged man, who had once more been reduced to a blurred silhouette due to the semitransparent wall of drizzle that had arisen between him and the car.

Still, the bloodshot eyes somehow seemed to retain their own light, even when the rest of the man's swollen face fell into the shadows. It was probably just his imagination, but that didn't make it any less frightening.

The cell phone lay on top of a thick pile of papers, and when Randall finally got control of his hands and grabbed it, the top sheet clung to his damp fingers and slid over the edge of the seat. It landed with one side resting against the floor mat and the other against the lower part of the gear lever. The paper was blank, except for the three words written in capital letters across the center.

THE LONGEST WAY. The title of the novel he had written the very last sentence of the day before. And the reason why he had been away from his home for the last fourteen days.

Endings were, for many writers, where the risk of writer's block was highest, and Randall had early in his career learned that this also applied to him. So, as a precaution, he had made it a tradition to head up north, specifically to a secluded cabin in Maiden Lake, when the final chapters were to be put on paper.

With trembling fingers, he pushed the screen saver away and tapped the mobile phone's handset icon. He then hesitated for a few seconds, mostly to gather his thoughts, before typing the three numbers that would help make the earth fall back on its axis.

"This is the emergency center," said a woman's voice at the other end. "How may I help you?"

"I'm ... um, there's been a terrible accident," Randall started, but when he heard himself say the words, he realized it sounded completely wrong. To call it an accident wasn't very accurate. It wasn't as if the man had just fallen on a bicycle and ended up in a gallows in the middle of the street.

"No," he corrected himself. "Not an accident. A murder. A man has been killed. He's ... oh God, he's been hanged. In the middle of the street."

"Okay," the lady on the phone said in an eerily calm voice. "I will send out a patrol car immediately. Are you at the scene of the crime right now?"

"Yeah, I'm parked by the intersection where he ... where he is hanging."

"Fine. Can you give me an address that I can pass on?"

Describing his location shouldn't be a challenge

for Randall. East Alin wasn't a very large town, and he had lived there most of his life, so he knew all the streets and alleys by name. Nevertheless, he struggled to identify the two streets he needed right now, and he ended up leaning to the side so he could look out the window and read one of the road signs.

"Wilkes and Kings Crossing," he said. "I'm parked at the intersection between Wilkes Street and Kings Crossing. In East Alin."

"Very well, it's been passed on now, and there's a car on its way out to you," the lady confirmed. "In the meantime, I would like to ask you a few questions."

"Sorry, what? Yes, of course."

"Excellent. First of all, I would like to know your name."

"Randall. Randall Morgan."

"And it's your own phone number you're calling from? In case we need to contact you."

"Yeah, it's my number."

"Good. You're doing fine, Randall. Can I ask you to describe the situation once more? In as much detail as possible."

"I ... um, okay. I was on my way home from Maiden Lake, where I've been staying for the last couple of weeks, and when I arrived at the traffic light here, I saw the man in the lamppost."

"And you're certain it's a crime? It couldn't have been—"

"A hundred percent."

"Okay. Was or is there anyone else around? Possible perpetrators? Anyone who is behaving in a suspicious manner?"

Randall glanced out through the rain-soaked windshield. The streets were empty, except for a couple who shared an umbrella a few hundred yards ahead. The rain and the twilight made it hard to identify any details, but he didn't feel it was necessary anyway. As dissolved and discolored as the hanged man's skin looked, it wasn't something that had happened right now, and whoever had done it was probably long gone.

"No perpetrators," he said. "He's been hanging out here for a while, I think."

"I understand."

After those words, the lady at the other end of the line paused to type something in, which suited Randall just fine. He needed to get his mind in order.

And air. More than anything, he needed some air.

He began to roll down the window at his side but quickly changed his mind as the rain had grown stronger and threw large, freezing drops onto his arm. However, he had to do something to dampen the nausea in his throat, so he leaned over the passenger seat and opened the window on that side. Enough to give him some air, but not so much that the script for THE LONGEST WAY was hit by the drops.

Whether opening the window was a good idea or not, he couldn't quite decide. Sure, it helped a bit with the nausea, but it also gave way to something else: the sound of the rope. The creaking, groaning sound of the rope as the wind alternately pushed and pulled the dead man. The sound seemed unnaturally loud, almost overwhelming, and even though he tried, Randall couldn't ignore it.

Out of the corner of his eye, he caught a glimmer of light in the rearview mirror. He turned around and was blinded by two large spheres of light dancing in the water streams running down the rear window.

Could it be them, already? he thought, but hardly had he completed the thought before the answer presented itself. The vehicle that now briefly slowed down outside his left side window, then accelerated and continued straight ahead, when the light turned green, had neither colored lights on the roof nor crests on its doors. And the driver wasn't a uniformed officer, but an elderly man wearing a red forester's shirt and a cap with the words: *BEER HUNTER.*

He really didn't see him? Randall thought while the taillights on BEER HUNTER's car got smaller and smaller and then disappeared completely between the buildings ahead. *He looked up at the traffic light. I saw him do it. How could he not notice the dead man dangling right next to it?*

There could be plenty of good explanations, he tried to convince himself. The man could be halfway blind, distracted, or simply so frightened by the sight that he ran off. Heck, he could even be wasted and on his way home from a bar. After all, he did have the words BEER HUNTER written in bold letters across his forehead.

It all sounded right but felt wrong. Because the man looked neither drunk nor frightened. He looked *indifferent*—and that scared Randall a little.

"Hello?" he heard a voice say, faintly and indistinctly, and it dawned on him that he had put down the phone at some point.

"Sorry," he said when he had picked it up again and placed it next to his ear. "I'm still here."

"It's okay," the woman from the emergency response center replied. It sounded like she was smiling. "It's understandable if you feel a little beside yourself, given the situation. You said there were no signs of any perpetrators. Does that mean you are all alone out there or are there other witnesses?"

Randall looked in the direction of the couple he had seen earlier. They were still walking under the same umbrella, chatting away, but they had gotten closer now. Before long, they would reach the traffic light.

"There is a couple taking a stroll out here. They are coming this way, it seems, but I don't think they have discovered him yet."

"And they're the only ones?"

"Well, there was a car as well, a while ago, but it just drove by."

"Okay," said the woman. "Listen, Randall, it shouldn't be long before the patrol car is with you. If you want, I will, of course, stay on the line until it arrives, but if not, then ..."

"It's all right," Randall replied. "There is no reason for me to waste your time. It's no problem for me to wait here."

"Excellent, then I would, on behalf of the police force, like to thank you for your call. Take care of yourself, Randall."

"You too."

With those words, Randall ended the call and put the phone down. Then he put his face into his hands.

He should have been home by now. He should

have been sitting on the couch with a cold beer in his hand and a huge smile on his lips because his latest—and most significant—book was finished.

The sound of voices made him look up. It was the couple with the umbrella—two young people, he could see now. They had reached the traffic light and were about to cross the street. They were heading directly towards the place where the man was hanging and would, in all probability, walk directly into his feet if they held the same direction.

Randall leaned over towards the open window in the passenger side to warn them, but by the time he opened his mouth, they had already reached the lamppost.

And what happened next closed up Randall's throat completely, so no words would have been able to pass.

For as the young man, holding the umbrella over himself and his companion, felt it bump against the hanging man's sneakers, he just pulled it down a little and tilted it to the left, so it went free.

And then they simply walked on as if nothing had happened.

— 2 —

The arrival of the patrol car was in many ways what one would describe as undramatic. There were no sirens, no blue flashes, and no sound of squealing tires. Had he not been waiting for it, Randall probably wouldn't have noticed at all when it snuck up behind his car.

The same couldn't quite be said of the officer. He spared no expense on the drama when he stepped out of the car. The door was slammed shut behind him, the asphalt got a heavy and slimy bullet of spit, and then he strolled over to Randall's side window with his thumbs hooked on either side of the buckle in the belt that held his pants—and his handgun—in place.

He was a big man; so big that Randall had to lean close to the window to be able to look all the way up to his face. It didn't help much, however, as the brim of the officer's hat left everything but his wide chin in the dark.

With a hand that looked able to pulverize a golf ball without much effort, the officer knocked on the window and signaled Randall to roll it down. When that was done, he leaned down and looked at him.

"Randall Morgan?" he asked, and when Randall nodded, he did the same. "You called 911?"

Randall nodded once more and kept staring at the big man in anticipation. Apparently, though, that dry statement was all the officer intended to say.

"Uh, yeah, I did," Randall said, pointing to the man hanging from the lamppost. "I called to report that."

The officer tilted his head and followed the invisible line from Randall's fingertip up to the face of the dead man. Then he wrinkled his nose and let his gaze fall back on Randall. A gaze that was devoid of empathy and only expressed mild interest.

He doesn't give a shit either, Randall thought, partly offended and partly frightened. *What the hell is wrong with people today?*

"We are going to need an official testimony from

you," the officer said.

"Yeah, sure," Randall replied. "I've already told everything to the lady from the emergency response center, but—"

"At the station."

"At the police station? Is that really necessary?"

The officer looked down at the ground for a moment, causing some of the water that had accumulated in a puddle on top of the hat's brim to fall off. It hit the asphalt with three small splashes.

"At the station," he repeated. "I need you to come with me to the police station to testify."

"But ... but what about him? Are you just going to let him hang there?"

"A couple of cars are gonna arrive shortly with some of my colleagues. They will take care of it."

Randall felt like protesting, but something told him that the enormous man outside the window—whose uniform was now so soaked by the rain that it clung to his muscular shoulders like an extra layer of skin—hadn't had the best day in the world and was just waiting for an excuse to take it out on somebody. Therefore, he limited himself to a polite nod, as he said:

"Fine. Then I guess I'll come with you to the station. Can you lead the way? I'll follow."

The officer rubbed the back of his neck and looked up to the sky for a moment. Then he bent down so Randall for the first time could see all the details of his face.

Maybe it was the skin's strangely smooth, almost wax-like structure, or maybe it was just the way the lips smiled without the eyes following suit, but something about that face seemed ... wrong.

"I would prefer that you follow me into the patrol car," he said.

"Do I really need to do that? It's not like I'm planning to run off or anything, I just ... hey, wait a minute. Am I under suspicion? Is that what this is about?"

"I'll drive you back to your car afterward, of course," the officer said, as if that answered all current and future questions Randall might have. "But right now, I would like you to come with me to the patrol car."

Randall forced his lips up into a smile he hoped

would hide both the anxiety and the budding anger he was feeling inside.

"Um ... okay, well then that's what I'll do, I guess."

He hesitated and then pointed to the cell phone and the stack of papers on the passenger seat.

"Can I bring this with me? I'm not too keen on leaving it in the car."

The officer responded with a small nod, sending another splash of water to the ground, and then started walking back to the patrol car. Meanwhile, Randall picked up the loose sheet with the title of the manuscript from the car floor and placed it on top of the others. Then he rolled up the entire stack and put it under his jacket, after which he got out, locked the car, and jogged to the patrol car, where the officer held a door open for him.

The back door. Of course. With all the surreal and scary experiences—too weird to be bullshit, as his ex-wife probably would have said—Randall's life had offered him over the last half hour, it really shouldn't come as a surprise that it would be the back seat that he was offered.

That didn't mean, however, that the desire to take a seat in there was in any way overwhelming. He just didn't really see any other choice.

At least there was some kind of light at the end of the tunnel, as there had to be someone at the police station who would at least take him—and the whole situation—seriously.

— 3 —

"I really didn't have anything to do with it," Randall said as the police officer sat down in the driver's seat and fastened his seatbelt. "You do know that, right?"

The big man caught his eyes in the rearview mirror and nodded.

"So you've said."

"Good, it's just ... I just want to make sure I'm not under suspicion, because I really had nothing to do with it."

"Of course not."

"Actually, it wouldn't even have been possible for me to do it at all, because I've spent the last two weeks in Maiden Lake, and you saw what he looked like, didn't you? He's been hanging out there for a long time, and I only came back to East Alin tonight. I'm an author, you see, and I always rent a cabin up by the lake when I'm writing the end of a new book."

Would you just shut up? Randall's inner voice said, while the outer one merrily kept on speaking. *If you keep blabbering like that, he's definitely gonna start suspecting you.*

It wasn't the first time in his life he had had a similar thought. In fact, he was (if anyone should decide to ask) able to give the exact date for the last time he reprimanded himself for the same behavior.

First of September, eight years ago—the day he finally hit the jackpot and got signed at an editorial with his first book contract. An event he and Allie celebrated with a late lunch down by the pier. Well, *lunch* was perhaps a strong word, considering that the content of the basket they had brought in its entirety consisted of a blanket, a bottle of champagne, two wine glasses, and a bag of frozen peas which they found in the freezer—and which was only brought to keep the drinks cold.

Truth be told, neither he nor his ex-wife drank very much, and when they were pulled over by the police on the way home a few hours later, neither of them had consumed more than a single glass.

Nevertheless, the sight of the policeman's uniform that day had Randall resorting to the same idiotic strategy as now. He chattered. Babbled and ranted until he managed to turn a routine check into an alcohol test, with breathalyzers and the works.

However, the officer sitting in front of him right now, on the other side of a protective metal grid, didn't appear to be affected in either direction by his explanations. In fact, it seemed he couldn't care less. His primary focus appeared to be on keeping up the rhythm that the fingers of his left hand drummed on the edge of the steering wheel while the right one put the car into gear.

Outside, Randall saw the hanged man's eerily dissolved face slide by and then fade away behind the veil of rain. Shortly after, it was completely out of sight ... but he wasn't sure it would ever be out of mind.

He jumped in his seat when a shrill, metallic screech suddenly resounded in the vehicle. For a moment he thought the car's rims might have scraped against the curb of the sidewalk, but then he discovered the real reason: the officer had turned on the radio and was now holding the walkie-talkie up in front of him.

"B-3 here. Are you there, Dolores?"

There was a small pause—which the officer filled with another drum solo on the steering wheel. Then a female voice came in through the speaker.

"I'm here, Jim. Where are you at?"

"On the way back with the witness who reported a hanging tonight."

"Oh yes. Out on Ferguson's, right?"

The officer's fingers stopped abruptly on the steering wheel, and he glanced over at Randall, as if to check whether he was listening in.

"No, not Ferguson's. The intersection of Wilkes and Kings Crossing."

"Oh, I'm sorry, Jim. My bad."

"No harm done; we are already in the car. Where do you want me to go?"

"Give me a moment," said the lady on the radio. "I'll check with the other units and get back to you."

Following those words, another metallic click sounded, and then the car was again filled with silence. A silence that triggered an almost instantaneous migraine in Randall's head because his thoughts were given free rein.

For so much was happening at once right now, and he was having a hard time making sense of any of it. The hanging man, the couple with the umbrella, the man with the BEER HUNTER cap, the officer's cold insistence on taking him to the station … and now this bizarre conversation over the police radio.

Knowing that it might turn out to be a bad decision, he reached out and tapped gently on the metal grid between the car's front and rear seats.

The officer put his right fist down on his thigh and turned his upper body around to make eye contact with him. His eyes were narrowed, the pupils so small that they could hardly be seen.

"Now what?"

"Sorry, it's just … I couldn't help but overhear the conversation and I was under the impression that we were on our way to the station."

"You're a bit of a snoop, huh?"

"What? No, I'm just a little confused, that's all.

It's just that I ..."

"A real little snoopy doopy."

"N-no, I ..."

Now the officer's lips parted into a wide smile, and a dry, croaking laugh slipped out between them.

"Take it easy, Mr. Morgan," he said. "I'm just messing with you. We *are* on our way to the station. There has just been a little more unrest than usual in town tonight, so we may have to make a stop along the way."

Oh yeah, that's just fucking hilarious! World-class comedy, buddy!

Even though that was what he was thinking, Randall forced himself to smile. Mostly because the officer kept staring at him in clear anticipation of a reaction. How long he would be able to maintain that smile, however, he wasn't sure, for what had started as a confusing and unpleasant situation was now beginning to feel like a *dangerous* situation.

His rescue came in the form of a shrill click from the radio, which stole the officer's attention. With it came the sound of the same female voice as before.

"Jim, are you still there?"

"Yep."

"Okay. I spoke to Henderson and Carl. They were out on Saxton Road and Gibson Avenue with a couple of deviants a few days ago, so downtown should be covered by now. On the other hand, a couple of the major access roads up near Marshall's are missing. Could you possibly get a handle on 55?"

"No problem. We'll head over there immediately."

With those words, the officer ended the conversation and hung the walkie-talkie back on the holder. Then he turned the knob to the heater, which hummed for a moment and then sent a wave of hot air down the bottom of the car.

With the heat followed a sour smell; one that Randall at the same time recognized and had difficulty defining. Not until he leaned to the side so he could see past the back of the passenger seat on the right side was the mystery solved. On the mat in front of the seat lay a small, crumpled cardboard box. Across its sides, the same two words—MISTER NOODLES—were printed in an uneven pattern.

The sight of the box drew Randall's lips up in a sincere smile for the first time since it all started. There was something both comical and absurd about the idea of this officer chewing down those noodles. That this big, coarse monster of a man had been sitting with that tiny box in his giant hands. A bag of beef jerky would have been more suitable. But a box of noodles? No way.

From the box, his gaze wandered over to the sunshade in front of the officer's head. It wasn't open, but it hung loosely in its hinges and was gaping just enough for Randall to see what was sticking out of its built-in pocket.

"Is that your family?"

The officer looked up at the picture for a moment and then made a strange, humming sound that could have been a yes just as well as a no. Then he raised his hand and pushed the sunshade all the way up.

Whether this nonverbal response was due to it

being a sensitive topic, or the officer simply had grown tired of his passenger's small talk, Randall didn't know. But in the case of the former, he understood it all too well. After the divorce, he wasn't always thrilled when someone brought up Allie or Billy. Especially not in the period following Allie's announcement that she was planning to move—with Billy, mind you—to Newcrest, at the other end of the state.

At the time, Randall was terrified that the move would take a toll on his relationship with his son. And if he was being honest with himself, he could see now, a few years later, that his fear had been justified. *Botched* was possibly too strong a word, but calling his relationship with Billy *strained* would in no way be unreasonable or misleading.

He pushed the thought out of his head and instead turned his attention to what was going on outside the vehicle. They were approaching the center of town now, which meant more lights and more people in the street. Obviously, the rain meant that there were fewer than usual, but a fair amount had still decided to defy the weather gods by exercising their right to visit restaurants and bars.

Among these he saw a group of young people, dressed for a party and high-spirited. They caught his attention—partly because he was amazed that none of them had brought an umbrella to protect themselves from the rain, and partly because the leader of the pack wore an antler-shaped hat that flashed alternately with red and blue light.

With the flickering antlers as an unstable guiding star, the group ran from the nightclub they had just left to a large taxi, which was parked further down the street. Randall followed them with his eyes for the first stretch of road, but when they reached the intersection of Pineview and Saxton, something else stole his focus.

About a hundred yards further down Saxton Road lay Hillmoore, the city's largest shopping mall, which last year had acquired two of the adjoining plots with the intent of expanding. These two plots had since been transformed into construction sites with large, square metal skeletons. In the middle of one of the structure's corner crossbeams, a rope was tied.

At the end of it hung another man.

"Are you seeing that too?" Randall asked, and this time he didn't hesitate before knocking on the grid. "Tell me you see it too!"

The officer turned his head and looked down towards the Hillmoore mall.

"See what?"

"There's another one hanging over there," Randall groaned. "There is a man hanging up in one of the beams at the construction site."

The officer narrowed his eyes and then shook his head.

"Cement," he said. "It's a bag of cement, that's all."

For a moment, if but a brief one, the officer's dry answer had Randall doubting his own senses, as well as his own state of mind. But when his gaze returned to the construction site, the doubt was replaced with anger.

"A bag of cement? Are you kidding me? There's a man hanging right up there, in the fucking middle of town, and no one gives a rat's ass. There's ...

there's no one who cares?"

Only now, when he heard himself say the words out loud, did he properly grasp what it really was he had witnessed on this crazy night. Somewhere on the edge of his consciousness he might have already perceived the pattern, but at the same time suppressed and rejected it because it was simply too insane.

But where the man with the BEER HUNTER cap and the young couple with the umbrella could perhaps be explained, there was nothing to cling to here. No explanation as to why no one—literally *no one*—in a street filled with people reacted to the fact that a man was dangling from a beam over the construction site. They just strolled around, completely careless, as if nothing had happened.

You said it yourself, didn't you? When you told the lady from the emergency center that the man in the lamppost had been hanging there for a long time. If that's true, why hadn't anyone reported it already?

"Wait, are you just gonna drive?"

"It's green," said the officer, lifting his index finger from the steering wheel so it pointed towards the traffic light.

"I see that it's green," Randall said. "That's not my point. Why are you driving straight ahead? Shouldn't we head down there instead? What if he's still alive?"

"Mr. Morgan," the officer replied in a voice that clearly indicated he was running low on patience. "You have had a stressful evening, and it's understandable if you're a bit on edge right now. But I assure you—what you saw back there was just a bag containing some kind of building material. Probably sand or cement."

"You hardly looked at it."

This apparently was the last straw for the officer. He stepped on the brake—so hard that Randall just barely avoided a frontal collision with the grid's metal wires—and then turned around in his seat.

"Would it make you feel better, if we go back and take a closer look at it?"

Without context, the words he said were in no way alarming, but the look that accompanied them made Randall's stomach tighten, and even though he opened his mouth, he was unable to answer.

And of course, his silence just fueled the looming fire in the officer's eyes.

"Very well," he hissed, after which he threw the car in reverse and accelerated. "Then that's what we'll do."

With his pulse galloping away in his temples, Randall looked out the rear window as the patrol car backed in an uneven arc across the intersection they had just passed. It stopped briefly—a few inches from a fire hydrant on the sidewalk—and was then pulled forward and to the right at the officer's command.

Less than a minute later, it was parked with one of the front tires resting on the curb next to the construction site on Saxton Road—and here, up close, Randall had to admit that he *was* wrong. Just probably not in the way the officer thought.

It wasn't a man that was hanging from the beam. It was a woman.

As was the case with the man from the lamppost, this woman's face was discolored and dissolved—to such an extent that the skin looked like a Halloween mask that had been pulled crooked.

Her mouth was wide open, as if her last utterance in this world had been a scream. Out of it, tilted over towards the left corner of her mouth, hung a bluish-black tongue.

For how long this woman had been hanging there, Randall could only guess, but one thing was for certain: it wasn't a matter of minutes or hours. It was several days, maybe a whole week.

How the hell was that possible? Saxton Road was one of the busiest roads in the entire town, so how could ...

That was as far as he got in his stream of thoughts before a fresh thought tore it to pieces. A memory that came to him so clearly that he could almost hear the woman from the police radio speaking inside his head.

I spoke to Henderson and Carl, he had heard her say during her conversation with the officer. *They were out on Saxton Road and Gibson Avenue with a couple of deviants a few days ago, so downtown should be covered by now.*

It had to be a coincidence. The very idea that the police were running around lynching people was insane. Of course there was a logical explanation, and of course it was just a coincidence. Still, Randall felt the hairs on the back of his neck rise when he saw the officer get out of the patrol car and open the back door.

"Are you coming out?"

"No, it ... um, it's okay. I see it now."

The officer leaned down and stared at him as if to ask if he was sure.

Randall forced himself to meet his gaze and nod—and for a few seconds, as the big man started to get up again, he thought the tense moment had passed. But then the officer paused halfway through the movement, as if he had thought of something, and leaned down once more.

"Oh well, maybe not cement," he said, winking at him as if they shared a secret. "But you've gotta admit she was kind of baggy."

With those words, the officer reached in through the doorway and grabbed the back of Randall's head. Then he hammered it into the grid's metal with such force that the young writer's entire world was flooded in a tsunami of white light and pain.

After that, everything went black.

— 4 —

When Randall Morgan regained consciousness and opened his eyes, he found that he was no longer at the construction site on Saxton Road. He also wasn't inside the police car anymore. The soft seat cushions behind his back had been replaced with the rough, uneven structure of asphalt.

The world around him had also been tilted around, and what met his gaze when he looked straight ahead was the dark gray clouds of the night sky. From them, heavy, glistening raindrops fell in a constant stream down upon him. They were bitterly cold, and when they hit his bare hands, it mostly felt as if someone up there was trying to nail him to the road with icicles.

With a strenuous movement, he pulled himself up into a half-sitting position with one hand resting on the surface of the road and the other on his thigh. His head was throbbing, especially his nose, and he had to blink several times to be able to focus properly.

Now he caught sight of the officer. He stood fifteen, maybe twenty feet away, bent over with his back turned, looking for something in the trunk of the car. Like Randall, he was soaked, and thick jets of water fell from the tips of his elbows every time he moved his arms. With the patrol car's taillights as the nearest light source, these water jets had an eerie, reddish glow that made them resemble something else.

The thought of blood made Randall aware of the taste of metal and rust that dominated his mouth and throat. And it also helped put everything back in place.

"You ... you hit me?"

The officer looked back over his shoulder, replied with a small nod, and then turned his attention back to his project in the trunk of the car.

"I had to, Mr. Morgan," he said. "You gave me no other choice."

Randall opened his mouth to ask why, but couldn't get any words out and instead ended up coughing a pink mixture of spit and blood onto the asphalt. The answer came, however, from the officer, who had just located the rope he was looking for and pulled it out of the trunk.

"You're a snoop," he said as he started to walk towards Randall. "A snoop and a deviant, and I had to calm you down. Otherwise, you would just make a lot of fuss and commotion."

He's insane, Randall thought. *He's insane and he's going to kill me.*

As if he had read this thought in his prisoner's head, the officer's large hands began folding the rope at one end and then wrapping it around itself, forming the unmistakable shape of a noose.

And he was humming while doing it.

Shaking, coughing, and drenched in panic, Randall tried to get up, but his legs couldn't carry his body's weight, and he kept losing his footing. Eventually, in sheer desperation, he began to pull himself across the asphalt, trying to escape. He didn't get far—a few yards, three at most—before he felt the officer's fingers grab his shirt collar.

One swift pull was all that was needed, and then the officer had achieved what Randall hadn't been able to. He was standing ... if you could call it that, when his legs didn't really carry any weight, and his feet were only in minimal contact with the surface of the road.

"Let go of me," Randall whimpered in a blurry, snorting voice.

The officer stared at him for a moment and then shrugged his shoulders as if to say: *Okay then, if that's what you want.*

And then, before Randall got the chance to grasp what was happening, his body was again given the responsibility of carrying its own weight, when the officer hurled him backward in the direction of the patrol car.

For a few seconds, Randall managed to keep his balance, and he felt a glimmer of hope that he could maintain his momentum and use it to run away. Then his legs started to wiggle below him, and the escape attempt ended abruptly in an encounter with the asphalt; first with his knees, then with his hands, and finally with his cheek.

Now he lay there—curled up in an involuntary fetal position behind the patrol car's bumper—on the rain-soaked main road, touching his face. The entire left side was burning hot, and he could feel the blood flowing in a gentle stream from between his fingers.

Behind him, he could hear the officer getting closer; small splashes when he moved his feet, and a constant scraping, which could very well be the sound of a rope being pulled across asphalt.

Get up! Randall ordered himself. *If you want to survive this, pull yourself together. Get on your feet, find a weapon and defend yourself!*

He looked—first to the sides, then up—and decided that the trunk, which was still open, had to be his best bet. A tire iron would be optimal, but he would gladly take what he could get. And something had to be in there with the amount of time that the officer spent rummaging around before pulling the rope out.

With a movement that triggered a cascade of white-hot pain in his right shoulder and upper arm, Randall grabbed the bottom edge of the trunk with one hand. The other one he placed on the bumper of the patrol car.

That way—pushing with one hand and pulling with the other—he managed to get far enough up to be able to look into the trunk.

"A real snoop," he heard the officer mumble behind him—and then again, a little louder: "A snoop. That's what you are, Mr. Morgan."

Finding that the voice was now much closer was frightening, but what really had Randall's pulse galloping was the fact that there apparently was nothing useful to be found in the trunk. A bag of dirty clothes, two blankets, a plastic bucket with fish food, stacks of old newspapers—nothing but soft fucking Christmas presents that were completely useless.

"Do you find anything exciting?"

Given the situation, the officer's voice was astonishingly calm. It didn't sound as if he was the slightest bit worried that something in the trunk would be able to turn the scrawny little writer into a real threat.

As an extra emphasis on that thought, it dawned on Randall that he could no longer hear the sound of the officer's footsteps—and when he glanced back, he indeed saw that the big man had stopped. It was almost as if he wanted to draw out the moment to increase the anticipation. Maybe he did.

"It's actually a shame," the officer continued. "If you had just behaved nicely instead of insisting on being troublesome, I would have been much more civil."

He put on an indulgent smile and shrugged.

"I might even have allowed you a phone call so you could say a proper goodbye to Billy before I tied you up."

The sound of his son's name made Randall freeze.

"How ...?"

"'For my son, Billy,'" the officer said in a solemn voice. "'My little bumblebee. May you, as it does, fly high and safe, even when ...'" He waved his hand as if to invite Randall to join.

"'... even when the world around you tells you that you can't,'" Randall muttered reluctantly, and when he had done so, the officer spread his arms as if to say: *Perfect! I knew you could do it!*

The quote was from the manuscript for THE

LONGEST WAY. The officer must have found it in the back seat of the patrol car, where Randall had left it when he got in.

The thought that this psychopath had held those papers in his hands, flipped through them, and read the dedication on the first page, for some reason made Randall furious. That this monster had defiled his work with his touch.

Because there was a reason why that particular manuscript had taken Randall longer to write than any other. On the surface, the book was a thriller, but in reality, it was more than that. It was a letter, a declaration of love to his son, into which he had put his heart and soul. A letter that—if fate would allow it—hopefully could help to rectify their strained relationship. And that the officer's big, murderous fingers had now groped it was almost unbearable.

In his indignation and anger, Randall found a reserve stock of willpower he didn't know he had, but also didn't hesitate to use. He turned around and started pushing stuff aside in the trunk until the thing he was looking for came to light.

His torn and bloody hand ached as he stuck it down the hole and pulled upwards—but he got the bottom plate lifted, and there it was, right next to the spare tire.

The lug wrench.

He grabbed it and pulled it up. Not so far that it came up over the lower edge of the trunk, and thereby within the officer's field of view, but enough to give him the space needed to get a proper swing when the time was right. For he was painfully aware that he would get one—and only one—chance.

He clenched his fist tightly around the cold steel. Now it was just a matter of waiting. Listening for the little splashes, when the officer moved his feet, and when they were close enough, then ...

That was as far as he got before something cold and heavy slapped down on his shoulders and chest—and by the time he realized what it was, the officer had already tightened the rope and pulled it backward.

— 5 —

During his third encounter with the asphalt on Highway 55, Randall Morgan saw the skin on his elbow—and three or four inches down his forearm—rip open. He also saw his hand release the grip on the lug wrench, so it flew to the right and ended up in a puddle of water close to the curb. Last but not least, he saw a car pass by the deadly scenario without so much as slowing down.

All three things were horrible facts, but none of them took up much space in his mind in the seconds after the officer had tightened the rope around his neck and pulled. What had his full attention was the thing that his lungs, brain, and all the cells in his body were screaming for in a common chorus—and what he was gasping for in vain.

"Stop that," the officer said as he, with the hand that wasn't holding the rope, pushed Randall's fingers away every time they tried to loosen the noose around his neck. "And stop squirming around like that. You're only making it worse."

In addition, he landed a kick in Randall's stomach, thereby forcing out most of the oxygen that the work of his fingers had provided. Then he tightened the rope once more and pulled the young writer with him.

Choosing the perfect spot for his macabre work of art was apparently of great importance to the officer, who stopped, when they had reached the sidewalk, and let his gaze wander indecisively back and forth between the two nearest lampposts.

From his spot on the ground, Randall watched this strange selection process—and attempted to use every second of it to draw precious oxygen in for his lungs and brain. He would need to think clearly if he was hoping for a chance to escape this.

And as the misty veil over his eyes slowly dissolved, he realized that there actually could be a chance. Because even though the tow ride had brought him closer to the lamppost, it had also brought him closer to the puddle where the lug wrench had landed.

After the officer had made his decision—and

double-checked it by pushing the selected lamp-post a few times, as if he wanted to test its stability—he turned his attention back to Randall.

"You stay calm while I fix this," he said. "In return, I will make it quick. Deal?"

Randall nodded and then curled up with his head bent, as if the eye contact with such a superior being was too overwhelming for him. At least that was what he hoped the officer would read in the movement. In reality, he was trying to hide where his gaze was actually directed.

How far away was it? Would he be able to reach it in time?

Maybe if your legs worked properly. But the way you stumbled around earlier ... can you even get up without falling?

The voice raising this question in his head wasn't Randall's own. It was Allie's voice—or rather; the sarcastic and caricatured version of it, that since the divorce had tended to interfere with his thoughts. Especially in situations where he doubted himself. This time, however, it turned out that it had something constructive to offer:

Wait until he pulls you up. Let him help you get on your feet and then kick him in the balls.

He looked up at the officer, who was now in the process of wrapping half of the rope together in a roll and then throwing it in a large arc up over the lamppost. The idea of having to kick this monster of a man—a person whose raw size alone would probably be able to secure him a place on a football team—wasn't very appealing. Neither was the idea of letting this man hang him without resisting. But no matter how unappealing it seemed, he did realize that the inner version of his ex-wife's voice was probably right. A good, old-fashioned kick in the crotch would be his best bet.

When he was satisfied with his makeshift gallows, the officer mumbled something to himself and nodded. Then he grabbed the rope with both hands and spread his legs the same way a weightlifter would before a heavy lift.

Knowing what the next step in the ritual would be—and that his timing in the seconds following would be paramount—Randall drew one last, desperate mouthful of air into his lungs, slid the fingers of both hands beneath the rope around his neck, and squeezed tightly.

The first pulls—not one as he had expected, but three in rapid succession—came far quicker and more violently than he had imagined. In just a few seconds he was so high up that his feet were no longer in contact with the ground. The plan of kicking the officer in the crotch also went down the drain. It ended up being nothing more than a pathetic twitch with his foot in the air to the right of the officer's hip.

For a terrible moment, he thought this would be the end. That the sound of the creaking rope would be the last thing he would hear in this world, and that the last black theater curtain would be drawn before his eyes as he hung there, eerily aware of his defeat and gasping for air.

But then, as the officer walked over to the lamppost to tie the rope—and thereby came back within reach—the goddess of fate opened a new window. And this time, Randall didn't hesitate to jump through it.

The kick hit clean as a bell on the officer's nose.

With the sound of celery stalks breaking in half, it was twisted sideways, sending a burst of blood across his cheek, while the rest of the big man's body staggered a few steps backwards, then sank down on the sidewalk.

And while doing so, he let go of the rope.

The reunion with the sidewalk sent a fresh wave of pain up through Randall's legs, and the noose was still tight enough to prevent any air from getting into his throat. Yet something—perhaps the adrenaline in his veins, perhaps the awareness that the weapon was suddenly within reach—gave him the strength to ignore both things and get up.

Stumbling and groaning, he traversed the three yards between him and the puddle, where the lug wrench lay, gleaming like a saving cross in the glow of the streetlamp. And as he closed his fingers around the two welded pieces of steel that it consisted of, he also had a moment of almost religious gratitude. However, that moment was quickly and cynically shattered when Allie's voice reappeared in his head.

Yes, that's very nice, Randall, she said. *You have a*

weapon now. But so does he.

Half expecting to stare directly into the barrel of the gun, Randall turned around. To his relief, the officer apparently hadn't realized that he still had his service pistol hanging from his belt.

Actually, he didn't look like a man capable of realizing much. He was still sitting on the sidewalk, in the same place where he had fallen after the kick, touching his nose. The eyes of his blood-smeared face were wide open, and his gaze was fixed rigidly on the ground.

For a moment Randall thought it might be the rope that lay in a curved line on the asphalt between them and still led to the loop around his neck that had caught the big man's attention.

But the officer made no attempt to reach out for the rope. It almost looked like he was staring straight through it.

Forget him, Allie whispered in the back of Randall's mind as he loosened the rope, pulled it off his neck, and then began walking towards the officer. *He's not a threat anymore. Right now, you're the victim. If you attack him now, that balance will change. So turn around and go home instead.*

The point was fair, and had it not been for the all-overshadowing anger within him, Randall might even have listened to it.

But the anger was there, and it had to be vented.

The first blow broke something inside the officer's forearm as he tried to fend it off. The second landed on his temple and brought him to the ground. The third ensured that he would stay there.

When the realization that it was over hit him, Randall let go of the lug wrench and sank to the ground next to the officer. There he remained seated for a while, while his gaze flickered back and forth between his own hands and the officer's bloody face.

For some reason, his brain found it hard to link the two things together. Hard to understand that he could have done this. And perhaps even harder to accept that he was able to lose control in that way and let himself be driven by blind rage.

At some point, however, it dawned on him, and with the realization came instant nausea that made him lean to the side and vomit.

When he raised his head again, Randall felt a little better. His hands were still trembling, and his heart rate was nowhere near its normal range, but some of the fog clogging up his mind had dissolved.

He placed his hands on the ground to get up, but then hesitated and moved them over to the holster in the officer's belt instead. It wasn't that he thought the big man would wake up again right away ... but should it happen, he saw no reason for him to have a deadly weapon hanging on his hip.

Very carefully, he opened the flap holding the gun in place. It was a bit stubborn, and for a moment he was worried that he would accidentally touch something and make the gun go off. It was silly, of course, as the safety would undoubtedly be on, but still he couldn't let go of the thought.

For a moment, once he had gotten the gun out of the holster, and felt its weight, he was tempted to take it with him. In fact, his hand was on its way around behind his back to fasten it in the waistband of his jeans when he came back to reality with a jolt and instead threw it into a big, thorny bush some distance away from the roadside. Even if the officer were to spot it in there, he would hardly feel the urge to crawl in after it.

Taking comfort in that thought, Randall took one last look at the unconscious officer, then got up and staggered over to the back door of the patrol car.

It was another silly thing, he knew that very well, but he simply couldn't bring himself to leave his book manuscript in the back seat of the police car.

For my son, Billy.

Yes, it would in all probability get drenched and ruined by the rain, even if he kept it under his jacket.

My little bumblebee.

And yes, he had made a backup copy online, of course. But still, the idea that the monster lying behind him bleeding on the sidewalk should ever touch those papers again ... no fucking way.

— 6 —

A little over half an hour later, Randall—drenched, exhausted, and discouraged—stood in the parking lot in front of Carol's Diner, staring at the large neon sign mounted on the roof. And at the man who hung from it.

As for places to eat in East Alin, Carol's wasn't at the top of the list. At least not if the measure was the quality of the gastronomic experience. Nevertheless, the diner was doing great—and had done so for decades.

There was a simple explanation, though, because Carol's Diner had an excellent location. Its nearest neighbor was the Pine Mill sawmill, which beyond comparison was the company in East Alin with the highest number of employees. And when the four o'clock bell rang at Pine Mill, a large portion of those employees went straight over to Carol's—often to stay there until they were kicked out.

That was one of the reasons why Randall had

come here. He knew there would be people—or rather *witnesses*—if needed. And there were people here. He just hadn't taken into account that one of them would be hanging like a creepy shadow under one of the neon sign's letters—and that the rest of them would be completely indifferent.

The other reason he had chosen to go to Carol's Diner was the phone booth on the right side of the building. Not surprisingly, the three hard collisions with the asphalt on Highway 55 had been too much to handle for the cell phone in his pocket. The screen had cracked in several places, and when he tried to turn it on, he got nothing but a soft metallic whistle out of it. Ergo, he had to resort to telecommunications of the more traditional kind. At least he found that he had some small change in his pocket. Because he wasn't sure he would have been able to enter the actual building. Not after seeing how the guests came and went, completely unaffected by the dead man dangling over them. Moreover, he didn't know whether the thing that was wrong with them was limited to the collective apathy, or if they might also be dangerous, like the officer.

In any case, this was something he neither had the energy nor the desire to investigate right now. Therefore, he did his best to avoid the most illuminated places in the parking lot while moving over to the telephone booth.

When he entered the booth and shut the door behind him, he also shut off most of the sounds from outside. Of course, the rain's drumming on the roof and the windows were still there, but the sounds of the diner—voices and the rattling of glasses and plates, mixed with Springsteen's *Born to Run* on the jukebox—died out almost immediately.

And there, in the moment where Randall's focus returned to his own thoughts, it dawned on him that he was facing a problem. Another one.

One thing was that he hadn't really thought any further than that he had to call *someone*—and that it couldn't be the police. But on top of that, no matter who this *someone* turned out to be, he wouldn't get very far without his cell phone.

Because yes, the phone booth enabled him to

make a call ... but it didn't have all his contacts saved, like his phone.

"Fuck," he sighed, leaning forward so his hands and forehead came to rest against the side wall of the phone booth. He felt like hammering a fist against the glass. He wanted to smash it, so he could stick his head out and scream at the damn psychopaths who were promenading around out there, behaving as if the whole world hadn't gone to hell.

Of course, there was one phone number he could remember ... but it wasn't a call he wanted to make. Besides, it would probably be in vain, as dismantling the landline probably was one of the first things Tommy did when he took over the house.

That thought was an excuse, not even a good one, and Randall knew it. Even though a couple of years had passed since he last set foot in his parents' old house, he had, after all, been out there a few times since Tommy moved in. And if the old red telephone with the curly cord hung out in the kitchen during those visits, it probably still did.

Reluctantly, but also aware that there were no

other options, Randall pulled a few coins out of his pocket and put them into the machine. Then he picked up the phone and dialed the number that once belonged to his parents and now belonged to his brother.

Eight long beeps came and went before a small click cut them off, and a male voice—obscured by either tiredness or alcohol—broke through.

"Yeah, Tommy here."

"Hi Tommy. It's ... it's me."

For a long moment there was complete silence at the other end. Then Tommy's voice returned.

"Randall?"

"Yeah."

"Okay, I didn't see that one coming. Why ... um, why are you calling on the landline?"

"It doesn't matter, Tommy. I'm in trouble and I ... I need your help."

Certain that those words would be met with a sarcastic comment, Randall closed his eyes and took a deep breath. But Tommy surprised him.

"What happened?"

He knows something is wrong. He's seen something

too.

"Christ, I don't know where to start," Randall sighed. "Have you been to town recently?"

"What do you mean?"

"I mean, if you've been in East Alin in the last week or so. Have you seen what's happened?"

"Well, I've gotten groceries a few times," Tommy confirmed. "But other than that ..."

"Did you see them?"

Now the silence returned at the other end of the line, and when the answer finally came, it was in the form of a new question.

"Did I see who?"

Had it not been for the nervous *what're ya raving about?* snort that followed the words, Randall would probably have believed that Tommy really didn't know what he was referring to. But the nervous snort was there, as it always had been when Tommy tried to hide something. In their childhood, it often accompanied the wild explanations offered when their parents asked about his school grades, and in his adulthood, it typically resurfaced when Tommy had fucked up and someone asked if he had fallen off the wagon.

So yeah, Tommy knew there was something wrong in East Alin, but he apparently needed Randall to throw his cards on the table first. And even though Randall was a bit annoyed, he didn't find it completely unfair. After all, the distrust went both ways, and he felt the same way.

"Take your pick," he replied. "All the hanged people, the police who are lynching them, or the rest of the town who don't give a shit. Any of that ring a bell?"

Another break, before the answer came. This time so long that Randall checked to see if there was still light in the display over the coin hole.

"For fuck's sake, Randall," Tommy said softly. "Yes, it does ring a bell. What the hell is going on?"

A relief, deep and intense, shot through Randall's body at the realization that he wasn't alone after all, and he had to concentrate to keep his emotions in check.

"We'll talk about it later, I'll be out of money soon. Are you ... can you pick me up?"

"Yeah, I'm sober, and I can drive, you asshole.

Where are you?"

"Carol's. I'm standing by the phone booth out-side of Carol's Diner."

"Okay. I'll get going right away."

"Thank you ... and Tommy?"

"Yeah?"

"Don't take the 55."

"Why?"

"I'll explain later."

"Fair enough. Stay put, Randall."

"Thanks. I'll see you soon."

— 7 —

After making the phone call, Randall's plan was to entrench himself in the phone booth and stay there until Tommy's Chevrolet showed up. In the end, though, it was the sight of another car—and its owners—that made him open the door and go out into the rain once more.

The car was a black Honda with the words *LIT-TLE PRINCESS ON BOARD—KEEP YOUR DIS-TANCE!* written on a sticker on the back end, and the owners were Joel and Kirsten Dalgas, whom Randall had known for most of his adult life. In fact, Joel and Kirsten were their best friends when Allie and Randall were still together. In their company they had spent countless evenings with excellent dinners and board games. And when things went off track with Allie, it was also Joel who listened to Randall's frustrations.

Maybe that was why Randall instinctively opened the door and stepped out when he saw them come out of the diner. Perhaps it was the memory of those evenings and of Joel's support during the most difficult period of his life that made him do it. The memory of how his buddy had dropped everything and was always on standby with a cold beer at the pool table in the basement when things got tense. Joel's calm logic and guidance had helped Randall a lot back then. Maybe he was hoping he could do something similar now. Make sense of it all.

Whatever it was he was hoping to achieve, it made him brave the pain in his legs and jog all the way over to the black Honda.

When he got there, Joel and Kirsten had just shut the doors, and both of them jolted when he put a hand on the window. However, the surprised expression on their faces was replaced with a smile when they saw whose hand it was.

While Joel rolled the window down so they could talk, Randall caught a glimpse of his own reflection in the glass. It wasn't a particularly nice sight. His hair was messy, there was an open wound on his cheek, and all around his neck lay a speckled, bluish pattern shaped like the braids of a rope.

But that wasn't even the worst. For behind his own semi-transparent reflection he saw Joel and Kirsten's faces. Their lips with the stiffened, weirdly insisting smiles and their eyes, which clearly recognized him ... but in no way seemed to register that he looked like an extra from a zombie movie.

"Hey there, Randall. Long time, no see."

Joel's deep voice, which was usually warm and had a pleasant, drawly Southern accent because he was originally from Texas, sounded eerily monotonous and toneless—and for a moment Randall felt so paralyzed by it that he had to concentrate to find the words.

"Hi Joel ... and yeah, it's been a while." He leaned down and waved to Kirsten in the passenger seat. "Hello to you as well, Kirsten."

"But I reckon you've been really busy writing," Joel continued. "We can see that you're practically spitting them out."

"What? Yeah ... yes, I guess I am."

"I still haven't gotten over the ending of *The Flood*," Kirsten interjected from the passenger seat—with the same lack of tonal expression in her voice as her husband. "You really got me with that one, I tell ya. That the boy turned out to be the one behind it all."

Randall tried to respond with a polite smile, but managed nothing more than a strained grimace. Of all the things he had experienced that evening, this was in many ways the most terrifying. Firstly, the apathy was even more frightening up close, and secondly, it was reinforced by the fact that these were people he knew.

"What about the family?" Joel asked. "Are they enjoying the big city life in Newcrest, or are they starting to miss the smell of pines?"

"I ... I think they're doing fine in the city," Randall said. "Allie probably wouldn't tell me otherwise."

Joel nodded, still with the creepy, stiffened smile on his lips. Behind him, Kirsten did the same.

"No, I suppose she wouldn't."

Randall hesitated for a moment, and as he did

so, his gaze wandered back to the neon sign that alternately was highlighting the words CAROL'S and DINER—and the man hanging beneath them—in blue and red.

CAROL'S ... DINER ... CAROL'S ... DINER ...

Over and over they jumped, back and forth in blue and red, like the flashing lights on the roof of a police car.

Knock it out of your thick head, his inner version of Allie's voice whispered. *Nothing good is going to come of it.*

That was probably true. But the question burned inside him, and he could just as easily suppress it as he could stop breathing.

"What do you see when you look up there?" he asked, pointing to the sign.

Joel turned around in the seat and looked back.

"Up where? The sign?"

Randall nodded and Joel narrowed his eyes. Then he shrugged and looked over at Kirsten, who did exactly the same.

"Well, the A is a bit crooked, but it's been like that for years, so ... I'm not quite sure what you mean?"

"The man!" Randall cried. "The dead man, who is hanging right there, above the entrance."

Neither of them said anything, but he noticed that the rigid smiles on their lips slowly changed and turned into smiles of worry.

On your behalf, Randall. Not because of the man up by the sign. Because of what they're hearing you say.

"And what about this?" he said, lifting his torn forearm up in front of the side window. "What do you see here?"

Joel looked at his arm, but only for a fleeting moment before his gaze slid down to the watch on his own wrist instead. There it stayed for so long that Randall started to fear that he might have had a breakdown of some kind. Then Joel suddenly rolled his eyes as if he were more shocked at what the clock was telling him than he was at the sight of the many slashes and bloody wounds on his old friend's arm.

"Oh my," he said, turning his hand to show his wife the dial of the watch. "Did you know it was getting this late?"

She shook her head with the same expression of complete bewilderment, and Joel turned to Randall again.

"Listen, buddy. It was really nice to see you again, but we'd better get going," he said in his creepy, monotonous robot voice. "Dina has had a long day. You remember what it's like at that age, don't you?"

While mentioning his daughter's name, Joel pointed with his thumb at the back seat ... but when Randall looked, an empty child seat was the only thing he saw back there. Before he had a chance to ask about it, though, Joel was already in the process of rolling up the window again.

"So nice, Randall," he repeated while closing the last few inches between the top of the glass and the rubber frame. "We really should do something together soon. Say hi to Allie and Billy from us, okay?"

And that was it. The transparent glass wall between them was completed, and the car started rolling away, while Randall was left with a mixed feeling of confusion and powerlessness. A feeling that only grew stronger when he caught one last glimpse of the sticker on the back of the car as it drove out of the parking lot's exit.

LITTLE PRINCESS ON BOARD—KEEP YOUR DISTANCE!

— 8 —

When Tommy's Chevrolet drove into the parking lot a while later, Randall had again sought shelter from the rain inside the phone booth. There he sat on the floor with both knees pulled up against his chest and his arms resting on top of them. He was exhausted, and had he not picked up the cones of light from Tommy's headlights out of the corner of his eye, he might have fallen asleep there.

He should be relieved to see the Chevy, but after the experience with Joel and Kirsten, doubt was rumbling in the back of his head once more. Because how sure could he really be that Tommy hadn't been infected by the same thing as them? It hadn't sounded like it on the phone, but he could be wrong.

Now you better take a chill pill, he said to himself as he put his hands on the floor and pushed himself up. *He is your brother. For that alone he should get the benefit of the doubt.*

He opened the door, went out, and felt relieved when he was greeted by the unmistakable sound of one of Kirk Hammett's screaming guitar solos. Tommy was—and had been, for as long as Randall could remember—a fan of Metallica. And that it still was their songs running at full volume on the stereo, had to be a good sign. It implied that Tommy was still ... well, Tommy.

Another good sign was the expression on Tommy's face as he raised his hand to wave to Randall, but then froze because he caught sight of the man up in the neon sign. For there were emotions present in his face. Shock, fear, and discomfort—all the appropriate reactions that a normal human being would have upon encountering such a macabre sight.

When Randall had almost reached the car, Tommy turned down the music and leaned over the passenger seat so he could push the door open for him.

"Holy crap, it's pissing down, man," he said, as Randall sat down. "It's totally ..."

He stopped mid-sentence and let his gaze wander down over Randall. A gaze that, with about the same mirroring effect as the reflection in the side window of Joel and Kirsten's car, emphasized to Randall how awful he looked.

"You really don't look too good, bro."

This dry statement was neither emotional nor poetic, and yet it gave Randall a lump in his throat. Partly because this was now the third sign that Tommy was okay, and partly because he suddenly didn't feel completely alone anymore. He had found a companion in this chaotic hell.

"I know I look like something the cat dragged in," he replied. "I haven't exactly had the best night."

"But at least better than that guy," Tommy said, nodding towards the neon sign.

Randall stared silently at his brother for a moment, then raised his hand up and pulled down the collar of his shirt, revealing the marks on his neck.

"Shit, Randall. Is that ...?"

Randall sighed and nodded.

"I just need to catch my breath, and then I'll tell you all about it. Right now, I just want to get out of here."

"Fair enough. Anywhere in particular?"

For a moment Randall considered whether it would be a good idea if he picked up his own car, but he came to the conclusion that it would be too risky. From now on, he had to assume that he was on the police's radar, and in that case, they would definitely be looking for his license plate. If the car wasn't already in their custody, that was.

"Just out of town, please."

"Fine. We'll go to my house, and you can sleep on my couch tonight."

With those words, Tommy put the Chevy in gear and started driving. Meanwhile, Randall sat back and stared at the windows of the diner's facade. They lit up the night with a warm orange glow, and on the other side of them he could see an elderly couple eating a late evening meal in one of the booths. Behind them, a little higher up, sat a group of men—probably workers from the sawmill—on bar stools, chatting. And when the waitress now and then passed them on her way to and from the kitchen, they turned almost synchronously on the stools, tilting their heads at an angle to study the stitching on the back of her skirt.

It all seemed so normal. Almost too normal.

When they were well out of the parking lot, Tommy apparently decided that the break had lasted long enough. At least so it seemed, as he let go of the steering wheel with one hand and made a small *okay, now let's hear it* gesture.

Randall nodded and cleared his throat.

"I ... I was attacked by a police officer."

"By a cop? You? What the hell did *you* do?"

"Nothing. I reported one of the ... hanging people. A man out in the intersection on Wilkes Street. And that was apparently reason enough to give me the same fate. In any case, they sent some psychopath policeman out there."

A brief glimpse—the memory of the policeman pulling the rope out of the patrol car's trunk—shot through his mind, and Randall felt the hairs on the back of his neck rise.

"He didn't care, Tommy. There was a dead man hanging in a lamppost in the middle of the street, and the only thing he cared about was getting me into the patrol car. And dumb as I am, I did it."

"How were you supposed to know?"

Randall looked down at his hands, which were still speckled with dried red-brown spots.

"That's just it," he said. "Part of me knew there was something about him that didn't feel right. Before he arrived, I had seen a few others walk past the man without reacting, and when the officer didn't seem to care either, there was a small alarm bell ringing. But still, I got in his car."

"And he was the one to give you those?"

Tommy pointed to Randall's neck and Randall nodded.

"He strung me up, and it was luck, more than anything, that I escaped. But I don't think it's just him. I think it's the entire police force. When I was sitting in the back seat, I overheard a conversation over the radio, and I think ... no, I'm sure they're the ones who are lynching people."

Tommy let out a heavy sigh, causing some of his long, silvery hair, which had pulled free from his ponytail, to dance in the air in front of his mouth.

"It's been going on for at least a week," he said. "I

saw the first one down by the car wash close to Earl's last Tuesday. To be honest, I wrote it off at first to be something I imagined. That it might be a consequence of ... you know, my wild youth."

He didn't elaborate further, but it wasn't necessary. Randall understood what he meant—and should he ever have any doubts, it was just a matter of glancing at the row of uneven scars running along the veins on Tommy's forearms.

"I didn't report it," Tommy continued. "There were some people over there who said they had already called 911."

"And what about when the police arrived? Were they ...?"

"I was on my way out to Crowling with a package, and I was already late, so I didn't ... well, hang around."

So fucking funny, Tommy, Randall thought, sighing. *Hilarious.*

As if he had read this thought in his little brother's head, Tommy turned his face and his gray eyes towards him. In them was a gravity that Randall couldn't remember having seen before.

"I'm not trying to be funny, Randall. In fact, I've been shitting my pants over this crap. Hell man, I almost didn't leave the house all of last week—because every time I did, there were more of them. More of the hanged and more ... indifferent zombies."

The words were allowed to hang in the air, while Tommy leaned forward and pulled out the car's ashtray.

"Does it bother you?"

"No, smoke away."

"Hell, I was planning to," Tommy said, pulling his lips up in a crooked smile. "I just wanted to know if it would bother you."

"You're a jerk."

"Yup. Tell me something I don't know."

"I talked to Joel and Kirsten," Randall said as Tommy pulled a cigarette out of his shirt pocket and lit it. "They came out of the diner just before you came and picked me up."

"Were they also ...?"

Tommy made a circular motion in front of his temple, and Randall responded with a small nod.

"Completely blank. I tried to get them to look at the man up in the neon sign, but they were totally indifferent."

He hesitated for a moment and then added:

"No, it wasn't just that. It was as if they weren't able to see him at all. And the same with me."

"With you? What do you mean?"

"The way I look. I have cuts and bruises all over, marks on my neck. You said it yourself; I look like shit, and it was as if they weren't even *able* to see it. As if their brains just ... shut it out."

Tommy took a drag on the cigarette, exhaled two small rings of smoke, and nodded thoughtfully as they dissolved and were pulled out through the crack between the side window and the top of the frame.

"How far do you think it reaches? Is it just East Alin, or is it other towns as well?"

"Your guess is probably better than mine," Randall said. "I've been up at Maiden Lake for the last two weeks, so this is all new for me."

"New book?"

Randall opened his jacket and showed Tommy

the roll of paper sticking out of his inside pocket. Although *sticking out* was probably a strong wording. By now, the manuscript was so damp that it hung like a wet washcloth over the edge of his pocket.

"Any good?"

Randall shrugged.

"I can't believe you're still going up there. Don't you ever get tired of the same place over and over again?"

Randall responded with another shrug and then turned his attention to the side window.

Outside, the rain had gradually subsided over the last ten minutes, which meant he could see a little further ahead. However, that fact didn't make the view any less discouraging, for they approached the large sign at the town's border on the northeast side of East Alin. From it hung, of course, another man.

And as if that wasn't bad enough, the end of the rain also brought with it an addition to the audio side of the experience, as the wipers were still running at full speed, even though the windshield was already dry. This resulted in a monotonous and un-nerving scratching sound every time they tilted back and forth.

The sight of the sign made Randall cringe, but it also made him think more deeply about Tommy's question. How far *did* this reach? Was it just the town, or was it the county as well? Maybe the entire state? Or—and this thought made him nervous—maybe even the whole country?

"You got your cell phone?"

The question made Tommy, who had apparently also used the pause to dive deep into his own thoughts, jolt.

"What? Yeah, I do. It's in the glove compartment."

"Can I borrow it?"

"Who are you going to call?"

"Allie. You still got her number?"

"I believe so ... but don't you think you should wait until tomorrow morning?"

Randall shook his head, then opened the glove compartment and pulled out the cell phone.

"I know it's late and she's probably going to be

annoyed, but I need to make sure Billy's okay."

"Fair enough," Tommy said. "The code is 2379."

Randall entered the numbers and waited while the home screen—a picture of the Harley Davidson that Tommy had restored a few years ago—faded in. Then he pressed *Contacts* and scrolled down until he found his ex-wife's name. When he had selected it, he raised the phone up to his ear. And then he waited once more.

One ... two ... three ... four ... five beeps sounded before there was a response.

"Tommy?" he heard his ex-wife say at the other end.

"No, it's me, Randall. I just borrowed Tommy's phone."

"Randall? Why are you calling this late?"

Even considering the late hour, Allie's voice seemed unusually indistinct and hollow. In many ways, it sounded like Joel and Kirsten's voices had done earlier in the evening. And Randall didn't like that.

"I wanted ..." he began, but then he paused. Because what was it that he wanted, really? To tell her that East Alin's lampposts had been plastered with dead people? To inquire whether she might have noticed something similar out in Newcrest? To ask if she might have felt a little extra indifferent to the world around her lately?

"I ... um, I just wanted to hear how you guys are doing," he ended up saying, and out of the corner of his eye he could see Tommy shaking his head.

For a couple of very long seconds, there was complete silence at the other end, and Randall braced himself for facing the biggest shitstorm of his life ... but what actually happened was in many ways worse.

"How nice of you," Allie said. "We are doing fine. Billy is doing great in school, and I have just been told that I will be taking all the photos for Fairview's advertising magazines next year."

Even while listing these things—which for Allie had to be nothing short of fantastic news—her voice sounded monotonous and tired. *Worn* was the word that came to him.

"Well, that sounds nice," he said. "Hey, listen, Allison, could I maybe get to speak to Billy for a moment?"

That he used her full name was no coincidence. He knew Allie couldn't stand it when he did that. But the reaction he was hoping for didn't come.

"Oh, I'm sorry," she just said. "Billy is not here right now."

"What do you mean he's not there? What time is it? Half-past twelve? He's not home?"

Another silence at the other end—for a very long time—and for a moment Randall was thrown back into the parking lot at Carol's Diner. For a moment he saw Joel sitting inside the car, motionless and with his eyes locked on his wristwatch, as if he were paralyzed by it.

"He ... yeah, yes, of course he's home," Allie said. "It's me who's babbling. He's just in his bed. Sleeping. And he's got an early morning tomorrow. So that's why you can't speak to him right now."

Randall's pulse, which was already beating fast, got faster with every word she said. Especially when she accentuated the words *that's why*. That was Allie's usual strategy, when Billy asked her about something she didn't necessarily have the answer to from the start. She pieced sentence after sentence together, and when she reached a place where it made sense, she exclaimed—as much to herself as to him—that *that was why* the answer was what it was.

"Can't you wake him up? I really need to talk to him. It's important."

"I'm sorry, but you'll have to wait. I don't intend to pull him out of bed at this hour."

"Allie, please. I'm begging you. I ..."

"Call me tomorrow, okay? Then we'll see. I really need to go to bed now too."

"Allie, wait."

"Bye, Randall."

"Allie? Don't hang up!"

A soft click. Then silence.

"God damn it!" he screamed, hammering his hand down on his own thigh. "Fuck!"

Tommy stared at him in astonishment but said nothing.

"We're going to Newcrest."

Tommy nodded.

"We'll leave first thing tomorrow."

"Now."

"Tomorrow morning," Tommy repeated. "Unless you plan on doing it alone—and on foot—then you'll wait until tomorrow. And to be honest, I doubt you'll get very far in your condition."

Randall opened his mouth to protest but didn't find the words. Because whether he liked it or not, there was truth in what his big brother said.

"Of course, I could also just let you out here, if you'd like," Tommy continued. "Then you can find a good spot on the side of the road and use your thumb. See how far that gets you."

"Oh, just shut the fuck up and drive," Randall sneered.

Tommy raised his hand in a military salute as if to say: *Yes sir, General, sir*. His lips smiled while he did it. Above them, however, his eyes told their own story.

Tommy was—no matter how hard he tried to underplay it to maintain his cheeky facade—also starting to feel the real weight and extent of the madness that was closing in on them.

ACT 2
RIDGEVIEW

"Fasten your grip, mates!
Hear ye not the sirens?
They're coming for you."
— O. E. Geralt, The Tides.

— 9 —

With the exception of the empty pizza boxes, the crumpled-up beer cans, and the random pieces of clothing that were scattered all over it, the living room of the house that once belonged to Randall's parents looked like itself. The walls were still lined with the same faded, orange-red floral wallpaper, and the furniture—heavy tables and chairs in dark-stained oak—also hadn't been replaced after Tommy took over the farm.

In many ways, the same could be said of the air Randall inhaled as he entered the room. It was warm, heavy, and still carried the same tinge of tobacco smoke it had in his childhood. Except that the sweet undertone of vanilla that his father's Virginia pipe tobacco had was no longer there.

"I've put some dry clothes out for you in the bathroom," he heard Tommy shout from the kitchen. "There is also a first aid kit in there if you need to patch yourself up. In the medicine cabinet."

"Is there alcohol in it?"

"What?"

"The first aid kit. Does it have any alcohol in it?"

"Don't think so, but there is a Desert Rose on the shelf above the stove that you're welcome to use. It tastes like shit anyway."

Randall looked down at his battered forearm and then to the shelf, where, sure enough, there was a half-full bottle of whiskey with a picture of a yellow rose on its label. The desire to cleanse his wounds with its amber content wasn't exactly overwhelming, but he had the feeling that the consequences in a few days would probably be even worse if he didn't do it. Therefore, he went over to the shelf and grabbed the bottle.

With the whiskey in hand, he went out into the hallway and from there into the bathroom. It was pitch black in there, and even though the chain for the light was exactly the same one that had hung there throughout his childhood, it took a few tries before he managed to catch it.

The threads in the free-hanging bulb began to glow, and as it gradually lit up the small room, Randall put the whiskey bottle down on the shelf above the sink. Then he opened the medicine cabinet door and located the first aid kit—a small, white box with a red cross printed in the center of the lid. He took it down, tipped the lid off ... and let out a desperate sigh.

Two bandage rolls, a pair of scissors, three safety pins, a crumpled cardboard box with old patches, and—only God could know what it was doing there—a golf ball. But no alcohol.

At least there was a bandage, he tried to comfort himself, while gently beginning to wiggle his sore arms and legs out of his rain-soaked clothes.

When all his clothes had come off, he grabbed the whiskey bottle and unscrewed the capsule. Then he stepped up into the bathtub, took a deep breath, clenched his teeth, and splashed the first wave of whiskey down on the open wound over his right knee.

A bolt of pure, steely pain shot up through his thigh, hip, ribs and all the way to his shoulder as the amber fluid hit the wound. For a moment, the bare flesh became spotted with small, sizzling bubbles, and as they dissolved, a series of small threads of red began to pool down over his lower leg.

The pain was excruciating. So excruciating that he wasn't sure his hand would allow him to lead the bottle to the other wounds to repeat the process.

And it also only did so reluctantly. Reluctantly and shaking.

The second wave hit the long wound on his forearm. At first it was bad, but then he started to lose some of the feeling in his arm and that took the worst of the pain.

Once he had tended to all of his major wounds, he put the whiskey bottle down on the edge of the bathtub—within reach, he would need a drink in a moment—and lifted the shower head up from the hanger over the tap.

He turned on the water at low pressure and gently let the jets run down over his wounds. To his relief, the hardest part was over.

After the shower, he dried himself with a towel that Tommy had laid out. He then picked up the two bandage rolls from the first aid kit and wrapped them around the worst wounds.

The sweater and the T-shirt that his brother had picked out for him fit roughly, but the jeans were a bit large. That didn't bother him, however, as it meant that the pressure on the wounds of his legs wasn't too bad.

While he was getting dressed, there were three short knocks on the bathroom door, followed by Tommy's voice, clearly pulled up in a falsetto pitch to imitate their mother's voice.

"Now you haven't used up all the hot water, have you, Randy?"

"Oh, shut up," Randall replied, but he couldn't help but smile, as the imitation was spot on.

"Fine," Tommy said, moving his voice down to its normal pitch. "Listen, I'm going out to the shed to get some wood for the stove. If you're hungry, just raid the fridge."

Although Randall was a little hungry, he didn't go out into the kitchen when he left the bathroom. Instead, he grabbed his jacket and took it with him into the living room, where he steered himself directly towards the couch next to the stove.

Before sitting down, he brushed a handful of

breadcrumbs—and something suspiciously resembling a strip of dried pasta—off the cushions.

In front of the sofa was a small, six-sided wooden table, and when he had taken a seat, he grabbed its edge and pulled it a little closer. Then he opened his jacket and took the rolled-up book manuscript out from its inside pocket.

Driven by the same inexplicable urge that led him to bring them in the first place, he now began to separate the wet sheets of paper and lay them out on the table. For some reason, it felt like something he had to do.

"What are you doing?"

He looked up and saw Tommy standing in the doorway with his arms full of firewood and his eyes full of confusion.

"They were completely soaked, so I thought I would dry them."

"Don't you have a copy?"

"Yeah, but this is the original, and ... I don't know."

Tommy raised one eyebrow, stared at him for a moment, and then gave him a sarcastic smile.

"It's gonna be worth a lot of money on eBay someday. Something like that?"

"Something like that," Randall replied, both unable and unwilling to give the real explanation.

Tommy shrugged and walked over to the stove. There he squatted down and dropped the firewood into a wicker basket, which stood on the floor next to the stove. Next, he picked up two of the top pieces from the basket, opened the stove door, and threw them in.

As the heat slowly warmed up the living room, Randall realized that the shower hadn't been sufficient to compensate for the time he had spent out in the icy rain. His body still felt frozen to the core, and his hands were shaking a bit.

Apparently, Tommy had made the same observation. In any case, he only squatted halfway down to take a seat on the sofa before getting up again.

"I'll find you a blanket," he said. "And what about food? Did you get something to eat?"

"Not yet."

Tommy replied with a small nod and then disappeared once more out through the doorway between the kitchen and the living room. When he returned, he had a gray, woolen blanket hanging over his shoulder and a plate with a sandwich in his hands.

"You better be careful," Randall said, while Tommy put the plate on the table. "I'll end up believing there's something wrong with you as well, if you keep treating me like I'm some kind of royalty."

It was meant as an innocent remark to lighten the mood, but as soon as the words had come out of his mouth, he regretted them. Not least because he suddenly became very aware that they could still be in danger of getting infected by the thing that made the rest of town go crazy.

"What do you think it is?" Tommy asked as he handed the blanket to Randall and then joined him on the couch. "A disease? A terrorist attack?"

Randall shrugged.

"It seems way too organized to be a disease, don't you think? I mean, they behave differently. The police are violent, while the rest just don't care. If it was a disease, it would be more random, I think."

"And if it's a terrorist attack?" Tommy said. "If they've sent some kind of poison, like that anthrax stuff, out to all of the police stations, and then they've put something else in the drinking water that makes everyone else passive."

"And what about the two of us?"

"Immune," Tommy said, poking his chest a few times. "The Morgan gene, you know. Think about it. We're brothers, we come from the same pool. Have the same antibodies."

"Nah, I don't buy it."

"No, of course you don't," Tommy said, letting his gaze glide over the paper sheets on the table. "It's not nearly exciting enough for your wild writer's imagination. Then what? Aliens? An invasion from outer space?"

The comment—and especially Tommy's dry delivery of it—made Randall chuckle, and he almost got the bite he had just taken of his sandwich stuck in his throat. And as is probably the case for most big brothers, that just spurred Tommy on.

"Now that I think about it, it makes perfect sense," he said, drawing a large, dramatic semicircle in the air. "Aliens that stun the population so they can invade the planet, completely undisturbed. It makes total sense."

"And what do they want, then?"

Tommy threw out a *what're ya raving about?* snort and leaned back on the couch.

"To steal our water, of course."

"Oh yeah, of course. And the police?"

"Just as simple. The aliens have taken over their bodies so they can squash those immune to the poison without anyone daring to interfere."

Randall scratched his chin and nodded thoughtfully. Part of him felt uncomfortable at the thought of them making fun of something that was actually deeply serious and scary. But another part of him enjoyed it. For he had—whether he wanted to admit it to himself or not—missed moments like this in the last few years when Tommy and he hadn't been on speaking terms.

"Seriously, man," Tommy continued. "Just think about it. What would a strategically smart invasion look like?"

Randall opened his mouth, but before he could

say anything, Tommy was already answering his own question.

"You would pacify the population with some kind of poison, right? And then you would use the authorities—for example, the police, which people trust—to catch those who are immune to it."

When Tommy began his definition of the perfect invasion plan, both he and Randall had wide smiles on their lips, but as he got further and further through it, their smiles narrowed and turned into two thin lines. For the explanation—however insane it sounded—made a little too much sense. Especially when Tommy reached the last, crucial argument and said:

"It would also explain the hangings. I mean, what is the first thing a normal person does if he or she sees a person dangling from a lamppost in the middle of the street?"

"Calls the cops," Randall said, after which he looked down at his sandwich and discovered that he was no longer hungry for it. He put it down and turned to Tommy.

"Can I borrow your phone again?"

Tommy shrugged, then took the cell phone out of his pocket and unlocked it. He began to hand it over to Randall but hesitated halfway through the movement.

"Don't worry," Randall said, taking it from his hand. "I'm not planning to call her again. I just want to check something out. You do have Facebook on it, don't you?"

"Uh ... yeah."

"And you're friends with Allie, right?"

"I think so. I don't use it very much."

Randall nodded but said nothing. His focus was on the screen, where his fingers quickly found the Facebook icon.

The program started and it quickly became clear that it wasn't an understatement when Tommy said he didn't use it very much. The timeline on his profile in its entirety consisted of two motorcycle photos, a photo of himself wearing pink, heart-shaped sunglasses and holding a Budweiser, as well as a good handful of annual birthday greetings from the same people.

The *Friends* list was also cut pretty clean to the

bone, but to Randall's relief, Allie was to be found among them. The relief, however, was replaced by an icy dread when he clicked on her wall.

Unlike Tommy, Allie had always been extremely active on social media. On the one hand, the various platforms were a good way for her to attract customers to her work as a photographer, and on the other, she eagerly used them to keep in touch with family and friends. These two things were clearly reflected on her timeline.

But just over a week ago, the steady stream of postings on her wall had stopped abruptly for some reason—and this was the finding that worried Randall.

He turned the phone so Tommy could see the screen too. It took a moment for Tommy to register what he was looking at, but when it dawned on him, he turned pale and formed an unarticulated *fuck* with his lips.

"A little over a week ago," Randall said. "It fits pretty well with what you said, doesn't it?"

Tommy stared at his folded hands for a while and then nodded. Then his gaze moved up to the clock on the wall between the living room and the kitchen.

"You need to get some sleep," he said, and before Randall got the chance to protest, he added: "We'll leave first thing tomorrow morning. I'll pack a few bags with food and stuff, so we don't have to stop on the way, and as soon as the sun rises, we're out of here. Okay?"

Randall took a deep breath and nodded. He didn't like to wait, but there weren't exactly any other alternatives. Moreover, the look in Tommy's eyes clearly stated that the plan wasn't open for negotiation.

"Do you have a bag I can borrow for these?" he said, pointing down at the sheets of paper on the table.

"I've got something even better."

Tommy got up, went to a dresser that stood below one of the windows facing the yard, and pulled one of the drawers out. From it, he took a thick, dark blue plastic folder, which Randall recognized right away.

"She left that here?" he asked. "I was sure she

would have brought it with her to the nursing home."

Tommy gave him a smile that at the same time contained joy and sorrow.

"I'm pretty sure she did," he said. "At least at first. But I think she snuck it back here after you and I ... after what happened at the funeral, you know. I think she was hoping I would find it and then reach out to you or something."

"That does sound like her."

"You can say that again," Tommy said, laughing. "A real meddler, she was."

He tossed the folder to Randall, who opened it and began flipping randomly through the thick stack of plastic pockets it contained.

Tommy and him building a fort in the bushes down by the creek. Tommy and him in the back seat of their parents' old Ford with two giant waffle cones in their hands and equally giant smiles on their lips. Himself on a sled while Tommy and his buddy were practically killing themselves trying to pull him up a snowy hill.

Countless memories that felt close and at the

same time so distant that they could have belonged to a stranger appeared with every page he turned.

Most of the plastic pockets contained four photographs on each side, but at one point he came across one where there was only one picture: his father, sitting on a tree stump down by the creek, putting worms on his fishing hook.

He looked skinny. Must have been one of the last pictures of him.

"I still stand by it," Tommy said. "What I said at the funeral."

Randall, who had neither the desire nor the energy to start that conversation right now, nodded but remained silent.

"You probably think I was so high that I don't remember any of it," Tommy continued. "But I do. And I still stand by it."

"Not now, Tommy," Randall sighed, sending his brother a pleading look. "Not on top of everything else. I ... I just don't have the energy."

For a long time, Tommy kept staring at him with an expression on his face that Randall had a hard time reading. It looked like he could explode in anger or break out in tears at any moment.

In the end, neither of the two happened. Tommy just got up, picked up the plate with the half-eaten sandwich from the table, and went out into the kitchen without saying a word.

Randall remained seated for a moment, pondering whether he should call his brother back. But it amounted to no more than a thought, and when he got up, it was to take the blanket off his shoulders and unfold it.

With it as a duvet and the sofa's armrests as a pillow, he arranged his bed for the night and lay down on it.

His expectation was that the night would be tough and that he would lie awake until dawn, tormented by anxiety and fear. However, his exhausted body had other plans, and it didn't take many minutes before his eyes began to blink slower and slower. Until finally they closed completely.

— 10 —

Just how many hours of sleep he had gotten, when he opened his eyes the next morning, Randall had no idea. What he could determine after looking around, however, was that Tommy must have gotten far fewer. For during the night all the pages of the manuscript had been put into the folder, which now lay on the dining table. Next to it were two backpacks—one stuffed to the brim and one half full—which hadn't been there the night before. So yeah, his big brother had been busy.

With a body that felt as if all his larger bones had been wrapped in barbed wire, Randall got up from the couch and went out into the kitchen.

Outside, the sun was rising, and through the large window above the kitchen table, he could see that the first orange-red flames had caught on to the lowest clouds. Before long, the rest of the sky would also burst into flames.

Normally he would have enjoyed the sight, but

right now—when it felt as if some vile god had decided to literally set the entire world on fire—the sunrise just made him feel empty inside.

He went over to the fridge, opened the door, and let his eyes slide down over the shelves. The selection wasn't overwhelming, but he did locate some butter and a packet of sliced cheese. He brought these two things over to the opposite side of the kitchen, where the breadbasket and the cutting board were located.

As he stood there preparing his rather mediocre breakfast, he heard a door open and close again. With the sound came a stream of cold air that told him it had to be the front door.

His first thought was that Tommy probably had picked up some more firewood from the shed, but when Tommy appeared in the doorway, it quickly became clear that it was something else he had brought in from the shed.

"I don't know about that, Tommy."

Tommy looked down at the hunting rifle in his hands—their dad's old Remington—and then back at Randall.

"Don't even start with that shit," he said. "If we are going out there, we're bringing a weapon. And good morning to you too."

"Yeah, good morning," Randall said. "I'm just saying ..."

No further did he get in the sentence before Tommy had turned around and left the room again.

You're such a fucking brat sometimes, Randall thought, but he kept it to himself. When it came down to it, bringing the rifle probably wasn't the worst idea, even though he generally wasn't a big supporter of firearms.

"I'll start loading the stuff in the car," Tommy shouted from the living room. "Can you bring the last bag out? Then we'll drive as soon as you're done eating."

"Okay," Randall replied, after which he stuffed the last of his cheese sandwich into his mouth and chewed it while scrubbing the butter knife under the tap in the kitchen sink.

Afterward, he went into the living room, where he picked up the folder with the manuscript and put it into the half-full backpack. Next, he lifted the backpack, threw it over his shoulder, and moaned at the weight.

Christ, you'd think he packed for a wilderness trip in Australia.

The bag was heavy, damn heavy, but of course that wasn't the only factor that came into play. His body also wasn't in its best shape given the beating it received the previous evening.

For the same reason, it was also with extreme care he walked down the five steps between the terrace in front of the door and the gravel in the driveway.

"Do you need a hand with it?" asked Tommy, who stood at the door to the shed, trying to get the key and the rusty padlock to work together.

Randall shook his head.

"Nah, I've got it."

"Are you sure?"

"Got it," Randall repeated.

And he did. But only just, because when he lifted the bag off his shoulder and let it fall into the trunk of the car, the walk had drained him of so much energy that he was on the verge of losing his balance and following it down there.

"You just get in. I'm going to lock up the rest and then I'm ready."

With those words, Tommy disappeared around the house for a minute while Randall sat down in the Chevy's passenger seat.

When Tommy came back, he sat down in the driver's seat and put the key in the ignition ... but he didn't start the car right away. Instead, he turned to Randall and gave him a solemn look.

"Are we ready for this?"

Randall looked at his brother and then out onto the dirt road that connected the driveway of their parents' old, secluded farm with the outside world. A world that had always felt distant when he was out here—and that now did so to a much greater extent than ever before.

"Not at all," he said and meant it with all of his heart. "But let's just get going."

— 11 —

Logically, the opposite should be the case, but in many ways this new world they traversed was far eerier in daylight. In the beginning, Randall wasn't able to put his finger on why, but with each of the small towns they passed through, the explanation became clearer to him.

It was the people. Not the hanging ones, but all the others. Those who handed out packages, patched holes in asphalt, went for walks with dogs, painted walls, cut down trees, and drank coffee in small cafes as if nothing had happened.

One thing was that the daylight naturally drew more of these people out. But it also made them more visible and underscored how insane their behavior was. For in daylight there were no excuses. No explanations or doubts that could benefit them and justify how they could uphold their daily routines without reacting in the least to the fact that dead people were hanging all over the place.

And dead people there were, in abundance. They had passed through four smaller towns at this point, and each and every one of these had corpses hanging from lampposts and signs, as if they were in the process of decorating for some bizarre holiday.

And the smell. Oh God, the smell.

In reality, neither he nor Tommy had a great urge to cut through the towns, but there was simply no way to get to Newcrest without passing through at least a handful of populated areas. And what was worse: before long, they would also need to make a stop in one of them, because the needle in the gas gauge was getting dangerously close to the bottom.

However, Randall didn't intend to waste time on that concern until it became necessary, because right now they were moving through a quiet forest area, where there was a long way between both houses and public executions.

Hardly had he let go of that thought when Tommy spotted something that made him snort and exclaim:

"Oh, no shit, Sherlock. I think we got that figured out by now."

"What did we figure out?"

"That," Tommy said, pointing to an old, run-down wooden house nestled between a cluster of tall pine trees about twenty yards behind the road ditch on the right side.

The little house was clearly abandoned and had, judging by its appearance, been so for many years. Patches of dark green moss covered large parts of the front, and of the five windows he could spot from this side, there was only one in which the glass was still intact. In front, the garden—an over-grown sea of dry, yellowish grass, which at the wind's command waved back and forth in sync with the rusty iron rooster on the roof—was framed by an old, worn fence. It was, in other words, the type of house that gives young children nightmares and makes bigger kids challenge each other to enter.

But that was, Randall understood immediately, not the reason why Tommy had drawn his attention to it. What had caused his brother's outburst and made him point to the house were the big yellow letters on the roof. The graffiti.

DON'T CALL THE POLICE! it said. A simple message, cut to the bone—and one that he could only support.

"Who do you think made it?"

Tommy shrugged.

"I don't know. But I'm taking my damn hat off. It must have required balls."

"That's for sure," Randall said, nodding. "But why do it all the way out here? We haven't seen any of the hanged since Melville."

The answer came when they reached the peak of the elevation in the landscape they were on and could see what was on the other side. Because there, at the bottom of the hill, where the trees stopped abruptly as the ground changed from soil to rock, was a tunnel making it possible to pass under the railway and the mountain on which it ran. And from the signs above the tunnel's entrance hung not just one, but two dead people.

Beneath them, across the dark gray asphalt of the road, was another warning written with the same screaming yellow letters and the same handwriting as on the roof of the haunted house.

The words were also the same, but this time—perhaps due to the bigger canvas—the unknown graffiti artist had added an extra sentence:

DON'T CALL THE POLICE—THEY'RE THE ONES KILLING PEOPLE!

The warning made Randall feel scared and strangely uplifted at the same time. Scared because it made the situation more real. Uplifted because it confirmed that they weren't the only ones realizing that something was completely wrong.

He glanced at Tommy and only got a brief glimpse of his face before it fell in shadow as the Chevy drove into the long, dark tunnel. But the brief glimpse was enough to ensure him that his brother struggled with the same ambivalence.

"How many of us do you think there are?"

"Sane, you mean?"

"Well, yeah, I guess so."

"How the hell should I know? Not many, it seems."

While he spoke, Tommy pulled—with a mildly trembling hand—a cigarette out of the pack he had in the pocket of his shirt. A pack that Randall had seen him peel the wrap off when they left the farm—and which by now was almost empty.

"You're getting some smoke in, huh?"

"Yeah ... and?"

"Nothing. What do you say we give the radio another shot?"

Tommy lit his cigarette, took a drag of it, and blew smoke out through his nose. Then he shrugged.

"Don't see why now should be any different, but if you want."

Randall nodded and stretched out his hand, but then stopped it in the air a few inches from the radio knob. And while it was hanging there, his thought version of Allie's voice decided to join in.

It's a bit ironic, isn't it? she mocked. *You wonder why he's chain-smoking when it doesn't seem to calm him down. And yet, you keep turning on the fucking radio, despite getting disappointed every single time.*

He sighed and let his hand fall down without turning the knob. Because no matter how depressing it was, it was no lie. He had been disappointed every single time. Fragments of interviews, babbling revival preachers, and advertisements for a wide range of products that one couldn't live without, he had heard lots of ... but on none of the many channels he had flipped through, had there been signs of anything being wrong. No news broadcasts reported on hangings or mysterious cases of apathy in the population. Everything sounded nauseatingly normal.

"How is the little bumblebee doing?" Tommy asked as the Chevy rolled out of the tunnel's darkness and into the light on the other side. "I've been meaning to ask. He must have grown a lot since I last saw him, I guess."

That he used Billy's nickname was completely natural. Everyone in the family had done so since the birthday party, where the boy, who had just learned to speak, spotted a bumblebee out in the garden and asked what it was, and then, when he had gotten the answer, pointed to it and exclaimed: *BumbleBilly!*

Completely natural. Still, Randall had to take a moment to get the image of the officer's condescending smile out of his head.

For my son, Billy. My little bumblebee.

"Yeah, he's gotten pretty big," he said, raising his hand so it rested in the air just below his chest. "About here. Maybe a little taller."

"Seriously?"

Randall nodded and Tommy let out a small whistling sound.

"Time flies, huh?"

His voice had a mushy tone, which made Randall feel a twinge of remorse that he hadn't tried to restore their strained relationship earlier. Despite his faults and shortcomings, Tommy had always been an excellent uncle to Billy, after all—and it had to have been a hard blow for him when he suddenly couldn't see him anymore.

"What about the new school?" Tommy asked. "Does he like it there?"

"I think so."

"You *think* so?"

Randall shrugged his shoulders.

"He ... we haven't really talked about it much."

That's a mild interpretation, don't you think, Ran-

dall? Allie interjected in his thoughts. *You haven't really talked much, period, would probably have been more precise.*

Tommy opened his mouth as if he had another question, but then closed it again and stared at something in the distance instead. First with squinting and then with wide-open eyes.

"He's been pretty busy, huh?"

Randall followed his gaze and felt his own face contract in disbelief in the same way that Tommy's face had done.

Somewhere between five and ten miles ahead lay the city where they would make their next stop. The road to it was fairly straight and cut through a checkered pattern of farmland in green and yellow colors that had to be an impressive sight if viewed from above.

Across the fields were scattered buildings; stables, silos and large wooden signs ... and the vast majority of them carried large yellow letters with different versions of the same message:

DON'T CALL THE POLICE!

IT'S THE COPS KILLING PEOPLE!

DON'T TRUST THE POLICE!

"Maybe we should try to find another way," Randall said. "It seems to be pretty bad here."

"Sorry," Tommy replied, tapping his finger on the glass in front of the gas meter's warning light, which was now on. "I'm not loving it either, believe me, but it's the closest city ... and probably the only one we're able to get to."

Randall nodded and then took another look at the many graffiti warnings adorning the landscape on both sides of the road.

"Yeah, well," he sighed. "We can't say we haven't been warned."

— 12 —

When Tommy's Chevrolet passed the big city sign—which in addition to bidding guests *WELCOME TO RIDGEVIEW; HOME OF RIDGEVIEW ROLLERS* also proclaimed that *THE POLICE ARE KILLING INNOCENT PEOPLE!*—it soon became clear that Randall's assumption had been correct.

It *was* bad here. Worse than any of the other places they had passed on the way here. Where in East Alin and the other towns people were only hanged at strategically selected places, such as major roads, there was no apparent system in Ridgeview.

The dead hung from lampposts and signs, just as they had in East Alin, but they also lay on lawns and sidewalks. It was as if someone had started with the same organized plan for the work, but then had given up at some point along the way and decided that it would be sufficient to scatter the corpses randomly all over the place. Or maybe they had just run out of rope.

Nevertheless, the apathy seemed to reign here in the same way as the other places. While driving through the southern part of the city, they saw several people navigating around the victims of the massacre, showing neither interest nor fear or disgust.

One of these people especially —the gardener on the tractor—gave Randall the chills.

The man was old—if not already of retirement age, then very close. At first glance he was a nice older gentleman with a silver-gray beard and a cap in the same green and yellow colors as the John Deere tractor beneath him.

Whether he was in fact employed as a gardener at Ridgeview Elementary or simply worked as a volunteer at the school was hard to say, but in any case, the man was preoccupied with mowing the grass at the sports field belonging to the school.

Three-quarters of the football field's grass he had already been over, and clearly this was a man who took pride in his work. The grass was cut evenly in height, and even in the difficult places around the goalposts, there were almost no loose blades of grass that had escaped the knives of the mower.

The same was true of the three places on the lawn where the dead people lay. None of them seemed to have been hit by the blade, and yet the man on the garden tractor had managed to cut very closely to them.

"Holy fuck, man," Tommy exclaimed as his gaze also found its way to the sports field. "And I thought Mr. Jansson at our school was bad. Can you imagine going out for a gym class and then seeing that?"

Whether it was an attempt to be funny was hard to determine, because Tommy's voice sounded hollow and empty. Either way, Randall found nothing entertaining in this. It was just sick. Nauseatingly sick.

There was something else as well that bothered him about what was going on at the sports field. Something he sensed beneath the surface of his consciousness, but just couldn't quite grasp. Some kind of dark realization that was just out of his reach and could only be glimpsed as it swam past.

Shortly after—triggered by a traffic sign with the silhouettes of two little girls and the text SCHOOL AREA; SLOW DOWN written below—it came to him.

The wording was different, but the message was essentially the same:

LITTLE PRINCESS ON BOARD—KEEP YOUR DISTANCE!

With the memory of the sticker on the back of Joel and Kirsten's car also came the memory of the empty child seat.

It was really nice to see you again, Joel had said as he pointed to it. *But we'd better get going. Dina has had a long day. You remember what it's like at that age, don't you?*

At the time, it was something that Randall only registered peripherally before it slipped out of his mind again.

But now ...

"Where are they?" he said aloud without quite knowing if the question was addressed to Tommy or himself.

"Who?"

"The kids," Randall elaborated in a voice he was barely able to control. "We've been through five different towns now. Six, if we count East Alin. And I haven't seen a single child in any of them. Have you?"

Although there were only a few years of age difference between them, Tommy's face—due to his dubious lifestyle—had far more wrinkles than Randall's. And right now, as they contracted in gradually increasing dismay as he pondered the issue, they made him look ancient.

"No," he said. "I haven't."

Randall looked down at his hands and then up at the street, where a red pickup truck passed them. He saw both through a veil of mist.

"Where the hell are they, Tommy? Where are all the children?"

— 13 —

Ten minutes later, Tommy drove his old, dusty Chevrolet in under the rust-red roof belonging to the Exxon station in Ridgeview, and parked at the middle of the three available gas pumps.

In fact, this wasn't the only gas station they had come across in the town, but the first one they had both rejected at first glance. Partly because there was a bit too many people, and partly because a couple of these were suspended from the roof above the station.

Here it was just the opposite. No corpses hung above them, and the only other vehicle they could spot was a moped parked in front of a pallet of gas cylinders on the right side of the entrance to the gas station's shop.

"I'll go with you," Randall said, as Tommy pulled the key out of the ignition and got out of the car to refuel. "Just in case."

Tommy grunted and made a sweeping motion

with his hand as if to say it was nonsense. But he still didn't protest when Randall pulled off the seatbelt and stepped out.

While his big brother filled the car's tank, Randall studied the inside of the shop through the large window in the facade.

No, *studied* wasn't the right word. He *analyzed*. Looked for things that could potentially be dangerous, noting the best route if they needed to get out again quickly.

In fact, it did look pretty peaceful in there. There were only two people: a young, fair-haired woman in her early twenties, standing behind the counter, and a teenage boy in a gray hoodie looking at bags of chips on one of the shelves.

Could the moped next to the entrance belong to him? It probably did. He seemed to be the right age for it, and the dark blue backpack hanging on its handlebars could very well be a high school student's schoolbag.

Behind him, Randall heard the gas hose being pulled out of the tank and put back on the stand. He took this as a signal and began to walk over to the shop entrance—slowly enough for Tommy to catch up with him.

Tommy would probably have caught up with him in any case, as Randall's body still wasn't exactly fit for a fight—and five stiff hours with his butt firmly planted on a car seat hadn't exactly helped on that account.

When the glass doors slid aside and let them into the store, they headed directly over to the counter, where they were greeted with a stiff smile from the clerk. A smile that—without him being able to identify exactly why—instantly told Randall that she was one of them. One of the blank.

The teenager with the hoodie he wasn't so sure about, even though he couldn't quite put his finger on why with him either. Maybe it was because he pulled the hoodie a little further down over his face and quickly disappeared behind a food shelf when they entered the shop.

"Gas on number two?" asked the clerk when they reached the counter.

Tommy nodded.

"Yup. And two packs of Marlboro."

"Regular?"

"Brown, if you have them?"

For a moment it seemed as if the young woman had fallen into a daydream and wasn't listening at all anymore. Then she blinked, pulled on the stiff service smile again, and took a step back so she could look down behind the counter on her side, where the cigarettes were stored.

"We only have the red ones."

"Fine. Give me two of them then."

The clerk nodded and then bent down for the cigarettes. Halfway down, she stopped to pull up her skirt a little, and Randall noticed that Tommy didn't miss anything. There were apparently some things even the downfall of civilization couldn't change.

While Tommy paid, Randall stepped back a few steps and cast a discreet glance in the direction of the teenager with the hoodie. He managed to get a brief glimpse of the boy's face, but not enough to decide whether he was like them. A *deviant*, as the officer and the woman from the police radio had called it.

He jolted when something suddenly squeezed hard on his elbow. He turned around and was met by Tommy's face, warped in a strained grimace.

"We're leaving now," he whispered.

"I don't understand ..."

Tommy put his finger over his lips and pulled once more at Randall's elbow, this time a little more gently so he was turned around and could look out the window.

And then he did understand.

Tommy's Chevrolet and the teenager's moped were no longer the only vehicles in front of the gas station. One more car was about to join them.

A patrol car.

For a terrible moment, Randall thought it was the same one he had been sitting in the night before. That the insane cop had somehow been unharmed from the beatings he received with the lug wrench, and had now found Randall again.

But it wasn't the same car. The crest on the side was different, the color was a different tone of white, and neither of the two officers in the front seats was the same man who had tried to kill him the night before. That man had been huge, and that was a category neither of these two uniformed men could be put in. Even the fair-haired one with the Magnum mustache, who by most standards was what one would call *in good shape*, wasn't even close to his massive size.

The only problem was that it probably didn't even matter. At least not if Randall's theory about the police being the ones behind the massacre held true. Then it made no real difference which member of the police force they were facing.

"Happy face," Tommy whispered as he led Randall towards the exit. "Happy face and polite small talk if we can't avoid it, okay?"

Randall nodded, but still found himself unable to pull his lips up in a smile when he stepped out the door and saw that the officers had already left the patrol car and were now walking in their direction.

He looked nervously over at Tommy, who with his eyes silently repeated the same message as before.

Happy face, polite small talk.

As the two uniformed men got closer, the doubt turned to certainty in Randall's mind. This was it. They would get caught now. Like dogs that smell fear, the officers would see through their charade, and then they would escort them to the nearest lamppost. Or maybe just shoot them on the spot.

But then, with only six or seven feet left between them, the policemen suddenly—and in an unnervingly synchronous motion—turned to the left and continued past them.

Randall saw them slip past and felt a fleeting urge to speed up and run the remaining distance to the car. He could see Tommy felt the same way. At least he was concentrating heavily on keeping a calm and natural rhythm in his strides.

When they had gotten safely over to the car, they opened the doors carefully and got in. And only then, when they had taken their seats and closed the doors behind them, did Randall find the courage to turn around and look back.

The officers still hadn't entered the shop. Instead, they had stopped to the left of the entrance where the moped was parked. They seemed very interested in the two-wheeled vehicle—and especially in the backpack on its handlebars.

Out of the corner of his eye, Randall noticed that Tommy had put the key in the ignition, and he told him with a small gesture not to turn it.

Tommy looked at him and then turned around in his seat so he too could look out the rear window.

"What are they doing?"

Randall opened his mouth to declare that he had no idea, but before he could say anything, the answer revealed itself as one of the officers grabbed the backpack off the handlebars and zipped it open.

After rummaging in the backpack for a moment, the officer pulled something up and threw it over to his colleague. The combination of the rapid throwing motion and the light from the midday sun's reflection in the metal made it difficult for Randall to identify what it was.

But the realization came, and when it did, it hit him like a blow to the diaphragm.

What the officer had found in the bag was a spray can. A spray can whose label was screaming yellow. The same yellow color as the letters in the warnings they had seen on the way here. The ones that said: *DON'T CALL THE POLICE!*

"Holy shit, do you think it's the kid who ... whoa, what are you doing?"

Tommy, whose hand had again found his way back to the key in the ignition, rolled his eyes.

"What do you think I'm doing? I'm getting us out of here."

"We can't just drive."

"We can, and we will."

"But what about the boy in there? You know very well what they're going to do to him."

Now Tommy released the grip on the key, but only to point a raised index finger at his little brother.

"Yes, Randall," he said. "I know what they are planning to do to him. And it sucks ... but it's not our problem. Our problem is getting to Newcrest. To see if *your son* is okay."

"And if it were him?"

"Who?"

"If it were Billy standing in there. Would you also just run away then?"

"That's not fair, Randall, and you know it."

"It isn't?"

"No, it isn't. Besides, there's not a whole lot we can do, is there? We're talking about two cops. Not just one, but two. Who both carry guns."

This reasoning carried some weight, and if Randall in the following seconds had kept his gaze directed forward instead of turning around and looking out the rear window, he might also have listened to it.

But Randall did look back over his shoulder, and when he did, he saw that one of the officers was now kneeling by the moped's rear tire and seemingly in the process of unscrewing the cap of the valve.

It wasn't hard to imagine what the purpose of that action was. Especially not when the other officer was at the same time keeping his eyes locked on the teenager inside the shop.

Turn around, kid. Put that damned magazine back and turn around.

But the boy didn't turn around. He just kept flipping loosely through the pages of the magazine he had picked up from one of the shelves, happily un-aware of the fate that awaited him outside the shop door. A fate which Randall himself had had a taste of the night before, and which he wouldn't let the boy suffer if it was in his power to prevent it.

"Tommy, open the trunk."

"It's a bad idea, Randall. Really bad."

"Just do it."

"Think about it," Tommy insisted. "You saw how many dead there are in this town. For all we know, those two cops are the ones who killed most of them. If you stick a rifle in their faces now ..."

"JUST OPEN THE GODDAMN TRUNK, TOMMY!"

Tommy sent him one last defiant look, but then bent down and pulled the handle that opened the trunk.

Randall took a deep breath, partly in relief, partly to gather courage, after which he opened the door and got out. Next, he walked over to the rear end of the car and pulled his father's old hunting rifle from the trunk. However, he only managed to walk a few steps with it before Tommy grabbed his shoulder and stopped him.

"Give it to me," he sneered, closing his hand around the barrel of the rifle. "You'll just end up shooting yourself in the foot."

Randall held his grip for a moment, then let go. No matter how bad he wanted it, he wasn't able to argue for a different distribution. Tommy was without a doubt the most capable when it came to firearms. After all, he had spent much of his child-hood shooting at tin cans in the garden with an air rifle. And, unlike Randall, Tommy had never hesi-tated to say yes when their father asked if they wanted to go hunting, once they had grown old enough to replace the air rifle with a real one.

"There's something wrong with you," Tommy said as he clicked off the rifle's safety. "You know that, right?"

Randall didn't respond, but simply lifted his fin-ger and turned it to the side to draw his brother's attention to the fact that the officers had now left the moped and were on their way into the shop.

"And still they say that I'm the irresponsible one in the family. I should have fucking left you stand-ing there in the parking lot at Carol's."

With this final, low-pitched expression of his disapproval, Tommy slammed the trunk shut, tightened his grip on the rifle, and began to walk towards the entrance to the shop.

— 14 —

Even with his own horrific experience from the night before fresh in his memory, it was deeply shocking for Randall to witness how quickly things escalated inside the shop. The two officers started no conversation and made no attempt to at least trick the kid into coming along voluntarily. At least not from what Randall was able to see from the other side of the glass doors where he and Tommy were.

What he on the other hand did see—with frightening clarity—was how one of the officers grabbed the hood of his unsuspecting victim's shirt and pulled him backward, while his colleague hammered a fist into the boy's stomach.

After the first blow, two more followed, causing the boy to sink to the floor. And once he was down there, out of reach of their fists, the two policemen started to kick him in turn.

Disturbing as it was, they seemed to find great

amusement in it, and they were so preoccupied with the project that they didn't notice the glass doors sliding apart behind them. It was only at the sound of Tommy loading the rifle that they turned around.

"Leave him alone," Randall said in the most authoritarian voice his trembling nerves allowed him to produce.

The two officers stared back and forth between his face and the rifle in Tommy's hands. At first with confusion dancing in their eyes, but then, after a few seconds, the surprise dissolved and turned into something else. Something that had a creepy resemblance to excitement.

"Seems we've hit the big jackpot today, Thomson," said one of the officers. If he felt the slightest bit intimidated at the sight of the rifle, he hid it well. "First the little rebel, and now two deviants."

His partner, the fair-haired officer with the Magnum mustache, nodded and smiled, but said nothing. However, Randall noticed that his hand was slowly moving down towards his hip, where his gun holster was hanging.

Tommy saw it too—and he responded immediately by aiming the rifle at the officer's chest.

"I won the junior clay pigeon shooting championship four years in a row when I was a teenager," he snarled. "Do you know how fast those things fly? Faster than your hand, that's for sure. Much faster. And if you as much as stroke that holster with your fingertips ..."

Virtually everything in that speech was utter bullshit. Tommy had never shot clay pigeons. In fact, Randall was pretty sure there had never been a single club, association, or competition for the sport within miles of East Alin where they both grew up. Still, the lie came easily to Tommy, and he served it with a voice that was impressively calm.

"Clay pigeons, huh?" said the officer, snorting scornfully. But his hand still pulled a little away from the holster.

Seeing him do that was oddly reassuring, as it implied that they—despite their insane behavior—still had an instinctive urge to protect their own lives.

"Let him go," Randall repeated.

The officer glanced down at the boy, who was still curled up on the floor between them, holding his stomach. He stared at him with the disgust that one would expect to find in a man who has just found half a worm in the apple he has already taken a bite of.

"You're just postponing the inevitable. There is no place you can hide. No one will house deviants like you."

"We'll take our chances."

While saying those words, Tommy took a step forward, thereby forcing the officers to take a step back. Meanwhile, Randall approached the teenager on the floor.

"Hey, kid. Can you stand up?"

The boy made a strained swallowing motion and looked up at him. The first few seconds his gaze was drowsy and unsteady, but then the confusion slowly dissipated, and he nodded.

"Good, then let's go."

With those words, Randall grabbed the boy's arm and helped him up. Then the three of them started backing out of the store.

When safely out on the other side of the sliding doors, Tommy pulled the car keys out of his pocket and threw them over to Randall. To do so, he had to release the rifle with one hand for a moment ... but at no point did he let his gaze—or the rifle's aim—wander from the officers.

Randall caught the keys and began to turn around, but was immediately slowed down as the teenager, still leaning on his shoulder, mumbled something incomprehensible and then tried to pull him in the opposite direction.

"What are you doing, kid? We need to go this way."

The boy shook his head stubbornly and pointed towards the moped.

"Sorry, but that's not gonna take you anywhere," Randall said. "Look at the rear tire. They let the air out before they went in."

"You don't understand," the boy sighed, pulling a little harder. "I need my bag. There's a pocket-knife in it. We can use it to puncture their tires so they can't follow us."

Randall looked over at the moped and then at

the officers behind the glass doors. So far, they hadn't moved an inch—but he didn't for a second doubt that that would change as soon as they turned their backs. Maybe it wasn't a bad idea to give their car the same treatment as they had given the moped.

Apparently, Tommy agreed. He caught Randall's gaze and nodded in the direction of the moped as if to say: *What are you waiting for?*

"Okay, kid, then take these," Randall said, handing the car keys to the boy. "I'll get the bag. Can you walk the rest of the way over to the car yourself?"

"Of course," the boy replied, but when he released his grip on Randall's shoulder and began to walk over to the car, it was on shaky legs that stood in stark contrast to his confident answer.

Randall ran over to the moped, grabbed the bag from the handlebars, and looked in it while running back again.

The knife—a small, red pocketknife, much like the one their father used to carry around on his keychain—was in the bottom of the left side pocket. It was a bit rusty, which meant he had to use force to unfold it. It also looked pretty dull. Fortunately, that was no obstacle to what he was planning to use it for. He was going to stab, not cut.

And so he did. The rear tires of the patrol car got two holes each, just above the place where the rim met the tire, and the rubber was thinnest. He also made sure to twist the knife's blade a few times after each penetration so that the holes became as wide as possible.

Feeling confident that the patrol car wouldn't get very far away from the gas station without pulling a tail of sparks behind it, Randall ran back to Tommy's car.

The teenager had already taken a seat in the back, but Tommy was still standing outside—and he still had his rifle aimed at the shop's entrance.

He stayed like that while Randall opened the passenger side door and took his seat. Then he did the same.

— 15 —

"Take a deep breath, kid. You're safe now."

That was possibly the exaggeration of the century. To be fair, the punctured tires of the patrol car meant that it wouldn't appear in the rearview mirror for the time being, but that didn't change the big picture. Civilization still sang its last verse, and the world as they knew it was still on its way down into a very dark abyss.

But hey, it actually looked like Tommy's remark made the boy calm down a bit. At least, the intervals between his inhalations got a little longer.

"What is your name, kid?" Randall asked.

From his spot in the back seat, the teenager stared at him for a moment with a completely perplexed look. As if he were having trouble remembering his own name.

"David," he then said. "I ... my name is David."

"Nice to meet you, David. My name is Randall, and your rifle-slinging rescuer by my side here is my brother, Tommy."

The teenager looked back and forth between them and then pulled his lips up in a nervous smile.

"Thank you for ..." He turned his head and nodded towards the rear window. "That back there."

Randall raised his hand and made a small *don't mention it* gesture.

"Why did you help me?"

"We could ask you the same thing."

"What do you mean?"

"We saw the graffiti outside of town," Tommy said.

"It was you, wasn't it?" Randall asked, and when he saw the boy narrow his eyes, he added: "We saw them pull a yellow spray can out of your bag."

The teenager made an *oh, like that* nod and then let his gaze fall down to his folded hands.

"It was me, yeah. I hoped it might make a difference if I warned people, but ... but it didn't."

"That doesn't change the fact that it was very brave," Randall said, and meant it honestly. "I'm not sure I could have done the same at your age. Or now, for that matter."

"I guarantee you he couldn't," said Tommy. "How old are you, anyway?"

"Sixteen. Seventeen in March."

"Are you from here? The town, I mean."

David shook his head.

"No, I'm from Gleamsdale. Or rather, I *was* from Gleamsdale, but now I guess I'm technically homeless."

"Homeless?"

"Yeah, I ... I ran away from home about a week ago."

Now Tommy turned around in the seat and let a skeptical look slide up and down the boy.

"I don't mean to be a smartass," he said. "But I spent a little over a month on a bench at the train station when I was younger, so I have a bit of experience in the field. And you neither look nor smell like someone who has been living on the streets for a week."

"Well, not homeless like that," David elaborated. "I've slept in motels. We had a piggy bank in the kitchen that was supposed to be used for a trip to Disneyland. I took it before I left, and it has kept me going so far."

"Does that mean your parents ...?"

Randall never finished the question and didn't have to. The way David's face contracted revealed that he knew how the last part of the sentence would have sounded.

"My mother, she ... short-circuited and became indifferent. You know, like the girl at the gas station. Only a lot worse."

We call them blank, Randall was just about to say, but it dawned on him that this probably wasn't what the boy needed to hear when he opened up and talked about his mother.

"I'm really sorry to hear that," became the alternative after a short consideration. "That can't have been easy."

David shook his head, and so did Tommy ... but then he narrowed his eyes.

"A lot worse? What does that mean?"

"That she ... that they get worse over time," David explained. "In the beginning, my mother was like the clerk at the station. She ... functioned normally in some ways, but at the same time she was totally indifferent to the stuff happening around us."

He let out a heavy sigh and shrugged.

"One day she was kneading dough on the kitchen table while they hanged a man in a tree on the other side of the street. She could see it all from the kitchen window, but she didn't even blink. She just stood there, kneading her stupid dough."

While describing how she kneaded the dough, Randall noted that the boy simulated the movement with his own hands in the air in front of him. It didn't seem like he was aware that he was doing it—which just made it even worse.

"But back then I could at least still talk normally to her once in a while," David continued. "As soon as the seizures started to get worse that quickly ended."

Both Randall and Tommy turned around and looked at him, but neither of them asked the question they both had on the tip of their tongues. They waited patiently until the boy answered it himself.

"She started to shut down for longer and longer periods of time. Trance-like, you know. And when that happened, you couldn't get through to her at all."

David scratched his neck and stared thought-fully out the side window for a moment, as if considering whether he should continue or close the conversation there. Then he met his own gaze in the glass and nodded.

"My father changed too, but it wasn't in the same way. He ... I think he's in on it."

"In on it?"

"Yeah ... well, he's not hanging people in the streets like the police, but I think he's been brain-washed like them and that he might be helping them in some way."

Before continuing, David took another break. One which clearly stated that he had now reached the most painful part of the story and had to con-centrate to keep from breaking down.

"And I'm pretty sure he took part in it when all the kids disappeared," he said. "I think he ... he helped."

It took a few seconds before the words sank properly into Randall's brain, but when they did, it felt as if someone had pumped his veins full of a toxic drug. A substance that his body was unable to handle and therefore made it tremble uncontrollably.

"Hey," he heard Tommy say in a voice that sounded like it was coming from the bottom of a deep well. "Look at me, Randall. That doesn't necessarily mean that anything has happened to Billy, okay?"

"But if something has," Randall exclaimed. "Oh God, Tommy. If someone has taken him ..."

"Then we'll find him," Tommy replied firmly, after which he turned to David in the back seat, who now held his hands apologetically up in front of him. "It's okay, kid. You couldn't know."

"I really didn't mean to ..."

"Don't worry about it. Instead, tell us why you think your dad was involved."

David stared—for a long time and very hesitantly—at Tommy, but then nodded.

"Because ... because I saw him do it. I saw him take our neighbor's daughter into the car when he came home from work one day. He just stopped the car out on the road, went into their garden, and lifted her off the tricycle she always mills around on. Without saying a single word to them, he just carried her to the car and drove off. And the neighbors were like my mother, so they just let him do it."

"Holy fuck," Tommy mumbled.

"Yeah, holy fuck," David repeated in the back seat, and in the side mirror Randall saw him wipe his eyes and then fold his legs up to his chest.

There were plenty of questions he still would like to ask this young man who had somehow found the strength to survive for such a long time alone in this hell. He just wasn't sure David's psyche could take much more right now. At least not if the talk continued to revolve around his parents.

"You've got no place to go at all?" he therefore asked instead. "No family in another city where it might not be so bad?"

David shook his head.

"I've got an aunt in Mellowfield, but I haven't been able to reach her."

"Mellowfield?" Randall said, sending a questioning look over at Tommy. "Isn't that close to New-crest?"

Beneath that question hid another, which he hoped Tommy would catch—and it seemed he did.

"Yeah," Tommy said and nodded. "It's not very far from there. You're welcome to stay with us if you'd like. Then we can swing past Mellowfield when we've been to Newcrest."

David considered it for a moment, then nodded.

"I would like to. Thanks."

"No problem, kid."

Thus, the deal was made, and although neither of them said it out loud, both Randall and Tommy knew that David could very well end up being a more or less permanent addition to their small group in this frightening new world.

— 16 —

"Do you have to do that?"

The words came out a bit more snarling than was intended, and as soon as he had uttered them, Randall regretted it. But the sound of Tommy's fingers constantly drumming on the plastic of the steering wheel truly was driving him crazy.

One thing was that the drumming disrupted the natural—and for Randall heaven-sent—period of silence that followed after they decided to bring David. Something else—and more important—was that the sound constantly threw his thoughts back to the police officer. That psycho had also been finger-drumming solos on the steering wheel during his cryptic conversation with the lady from the police radio about where it would be best to hang the passenger on the back seat.

Fortunately, Tommy seemed neither offended nor hurt by the comment. He just looked down at his hands for a second, then shrugged and closed his fingers around the steering wheel instead of tapping on it.

Behind them, in the back seat, David took an audible breath and moved a little from side to side. It was the fourth or fifth time he had done so in a relatively short time, and Randall was pretty sure the kid had something on his mind. Something he would like to say or ask.

Hardly had he finished this thought before David's face appeared between the front seats.

"It's your son, isn't it?" he asked. "He's in Newcrest. That's why we're going there, isn't it?"

Randall nodded.

"His mother and I divorced a few years ago. He lives there with her now."

"Have you ... have you spoken to him?"

"Not since all of this started. I tried to call Allie, my ex-wife, but she ... she didn't let me talk to him."

Because she's one of the blank ones now, a voice said from some dark place in his mind that he himself didn't control. *Because she's no longer Allie.*

For a moment he feared that David's next question would be about just that—and that he would then be forced to formulate some version of this thought and say it out loud.

But David went—perhaps consciously, perhaps unconsciously—in another direction and didn't dig deeper into the subject.

"How old is he?" he asked instead. "Your son, I mean."

"He'll be ten soon."

David nodded and shifted his gaze to Tommy.

"What about you? Do you have kids?"

Something outside the car had caught Tommy's attention, so it took a moment before he realized he was being spoken to. But when the answer came, it was in the form of a rehearsed speech that Randall had heard countless times before—and which was always accompanied by Tommy's trademark snort and a cocky smile.

"Maybe a couple of slipups somewhere out there," he said. "But I check my mailbox every single day and there haven't been any bills yet. Nope, I'm more of a lone wolf, you know."

That was the autoreply. The well-rehearsed smartass answer that Tommy always spat out—but also the answer that would cut a little in the heart of anyone who had known him long enough to know who Brenda Watson was.

Because Tommy hadn't always lived by that motto. Once upon a time, it had been his greatest desire to settle down and start a family. For a while he had even gotten enough control of his life to make people around him believe that it might be possible.

The only problem was that Brenda—the woman he planned to do it with—changed her mind at the last minute and ended up leaving him in a worse condition than she had found him in.

"Okay, cool," David said, but he didn't sound very impressed, and Randall had the feeling he also knew that Tommy's automatic answer was just a facade.

In many ways, he seemed to be a bright kid, which undoubtedly also explained how he had survived on his own for so long without getting caught.

While thinking this, Randall let his gaze slide up into the sky above them, where a small cluster of dark gray clouds had begun to intertwine among two others: like cars on a big, blue highway. Should it end in a collision, the glass of the windshield would probably get hit by the first drops before long.

Not surprisingly, there were no planes to be seen up there. This, Randall thought, had to be another one of the small, discreet signs that something was not quite as it should be.

He held out his hand, grabbed the radio's knob, and looked over at Tommy, who nodded.

"... which was originally written by Willie Nelson," said a deep male voice through the speaker as Randall turned the knob and turned on the device. "When we return after the news in a little while, we will continue our musical time travelling journey—and without revealing too much, I can promise it will be good. We are going to make a stop at the Woodstock festival, where a certain guitarist really made his mark. So please, stay with us here on WBCN!"

After a brief fanfare that had all the traditional hallmarks of a news program, a new voice now emerged. This time it was a female voice, and as one would expect, its owner spoke with the stoic calm of a newscaster.

But the words she uttered just didn't match that image—and for that matter, they didn't sound like they were directed at WBCN's listeners either.

"Just get her out, Jonas. What? No, she has no business being in here."

Whoever the radio host was having this conversation with, he wasn't sitting in the same room. This was obvious as only half of the conversation reached the microphone and was sent out on the air.

"Then call security and tell him that ... well, then call him again."

Randall's best guess was that it had to be the sound guy she was talking to. In reality, he had never set foot in a radio studio, but he had seen on TV that there often was a sound guy sitting at a mixer on the other side of a soundproof glass pane.

"Yes, but then she'll have to talk to management and get an appointment," the radio host continued. "We can't just ... no, you do *not* let her in here!"

In the background were some rattling sounds, as if someone had decided to give the entire studio a makeover in the middle of a broadcast. And not a gentle one.

"Yes, I can see that she is, but you'll have to stall her until the guard ... wait, what is she ..."

She got no further before the bang came. A bang that was so loud that it made the speakers in Tommy's car buzz and Randall's blood freeze to ice. After it followed the unmistakable sound of glass, shattering and falling to the ground. If Randall's image of the radio studio was correct, it wasn't difficult to imagine what had happened. Someone—probably the woman they were trying to keep out—had fired a weapon, thereby breaking the sound-proof window between the studio and the mixer room.

After a pause of nerve-wracking silence, the radio host's voice returned. It was lower and sounded more distant, as if she had moved away from the microphone, but amazingly, she still spoke in the same monotone pitch that didn't fit either the words or the situation at all. The pitch of the blank.

"You really can't be in here, miss," she said. "I beg you. We have some very strict ..."

"It's madam," interrupted another woman's voice. One that was full of anger and desperation—and for that very reason told Randall that its owner, unlike the radio host, wasn't one of the blank.

"I'm sorry, I'm not sure I understand?"

"It's madam," repeated the woman's voice. "Not *Miss*. They took Gerard from me, but that doesn't mean that this doesn't still sit on my finger, does it?"

"I'm sorry, madam," the radio host said. "But won't you please point that somewhere else?"

The answer, concise and clear, came in the form of a metallic click that could only be the sound of a revolver's hammer being pulled back.

"What is it you want?"

"I want ... I want my life back," said the desperate woman in a trembling voice. "But you can't give me that, can you?"

"No, I ..."

"So for now, I just want to borrow your microphone."

Another nerve-wracking pause followed, and then—far louder because it was now amplified by the microphone—the desperate woman's voice returned.

Except she didn't sound desperate anymore. She sounded focused. As if she had prepared every single word of the monologue she was about to deliver.

"I don't know how much time I have before they come and drag me away," she said. "It's probably not very long, so I don't intend to waste a single second. My name is Melanie Rosencamp. I come from Walkersville, but my hometown is no longer a safe place to be. The police are killing innocent people and hanging them up in the streets like ... like slaughtered pigs on meat hooks, and everyone else seems to have been infected by some disease that makes them blind to it. If there are others like me left out there, you probably know what I mean."

Randall exchanged a look with his fellow travelers and saw in their eyes the same despair and powerlessness that he himself felt.

"Three days ago, they took my husband from

me," the woman continued. "Gerard was ... oh God, he was killed. Murdered in cold blood by those who were supposed to protect us."

Although these words also sounded like a rehearsed part of the message she wanted to get out on the air, it was clearly hard for this Melanie Rosencamp to utter them. Her voice trembled and she had to clear her throat several times to keep it under control.

"I don't know why this is happening or how far it extends," she said. "But I do know that Walkersville isn't the only place where something similar is going on, and I think it's spreading somehow. So, if you're out there and you see something similar happening, make sure you get away as soon as possible. Stay away from the cities, especially the larger ones, and take ..."

She paused once more, but this time it wasn't because the emotions affected her ability to express herself clearly. This time it was something coming from the outside that made her stop. A sound that started as a faint rumble in the background and then gradually increased in volume until the elements, of which it consisted, could be identified: Quick footsteps on tile floors, agitated voices, and doors that opened and closed.

For a couple of long seconds, Melanie Rosencamp's voice remained silent, and Randall allowed himself to hope that she might have changed her mind. That she had decided to flee the studio after all while there was still time. But then she returned—and when she did, her voice was so calm and clear that it made the hairs on the back of his neck stand up. She had no plans to run away, and she had no expectation of walking away from this on her own two feet.

"Stay away from the big cities," she repeated. "Seek refuge in the countryside, and if you come across the police, then for God's sake, don't for a second think that they are going to help you. The guards are coming in here now, so I'm out of time, but ..."

Those were the last words from Melanie Rosencamp's mouth to escape into the ether before the connection was cut with a short metallic crackle. A few seconds later, the first notes from the guitar intro to Lynyrd Skynyrd's *Sweet Home Alabama* began to roar out through the speaker.

A live version, with resounding applause and cheers from the audience. Of course, it had to be a live version.

"Turn that shit off," Tommy mumbled.

Randall heard him say the words, but at first couldn't make head or tail of them—and when he finally broke free from the state of shock he was in, Tommy had already reached out and turned the knob himself.

The light in the radio display went out and the noisy Southern rock died out. But the silence that took its place wasn't necessarily preferable. In many ways, it felt just as loud and invasive as the music had been.

"Did I hear her right?" David asked from the back seat. "Did she say she was from Walkersville?"

"I think so," Randall replied. "Why?"

"Some time ago, we read an article in school about a group of boys from Walkersville who started a YouTube channel to raise money for the homeless. I remember the name of the town because we made fun of it, saying it was probably full of walkers. You know, like the zombies in *The Walking Dead*. You do know them, right?"

"I'm assuming you have a point with all of this, kid," Tommy said. "Because otherwise it's a pretty crappy thing to bring up."

Although Randall probably would have expressed himself a bit less harshly, he had to admit that he could only agree with his brother's position. A TV series about zombies and the end of the world wasn't a very uplifting topic of conversation, given their current situation.

However, as it turned out, David in fact *had* a point—and when he got to it, Randall almost wished that the kid had just hoped to use the city name as a steppingstone to an inappropriate chat about his favorite series.

"If it's the same Walkersville, then it's located in Maryland," was what David said. "That's 250 miles away from here. At least."

ACT 3
NEWCREST

"Click, clack. Click, clack. Can you hear it?
That's the sound of tiny shoes.
Are you scared yet?"
— O. E. Geralt, *Rats in the Cradle.*

— 17 —

As the day progressed and they approached New-crest, Randall gradually became more and more anxious about what he would find in the city. In many ways, it was like sitting on a bench in a waiting room, where the head physician could come in the door at any time with either very good or very bad news.

In this version, though, he was just sitting in the passenger seat of Tommy's Chevrolet instead, and the message wouldn't come from a man in a white coat with a clipboard.

It would come from the dead. If not the full answer, then the number of hanged people in and around the city would at least give him part of it. The dead would clarify whether his bad premonition when talking to Allie on the phone had been correct. They would tell him if the darkness that had sucked the humanity out of the people from East Alin—the same that, according to Melanie

Rosencamp, had spread all the way down to Walkersville, Maryland—had also infected Newcrest.

In other words, the silent voices of the dead would tell him whether the hope he stubbornly clung to was nothing more than a blind and irrational denial of the truth.

And so far, it didn't look too good. There were stretches where they didn't see anyone hanging, yes, but by and large the number had only increased.

Tommy felt it too. He didn't say it out loud, but the way he closed his eyes and let out a small sigh every time they passed one of the improvised gallows said it all.

On the right side of the car, a large, orange billboard rushed past. As he only caught it out of the corner of his eye, Randall only saw a few of the words written on the front of the sign. However, he had driven past here so many times before that he didn't need to read the sign to know what was written on it.

PISTOL PETE'S USED CARS—GET A YOUNGER MODEL, WITHOUT GETTING TROUBLE FROM THE

OLD ONE!

Actually, Pistol Pete's sign—though the man himself probably didn't realize it—had for a time served as a checkpoint for Randall. Navigating had never been his strong suit, and in the beginning, he often ended up being a little late when he had to pick up Billy on the weekends. At some point, however, he realized that Pistol Pete's eye-catching billboard was an excellent warning that the important right turn was coming up.

"You may want to slow down a bit," he said. "There's a road on the right coming up soon. It's a shortcut, but it's right after the turn, so it's easy to miss."

Tommy narrowed his eyes for a moment and then lifted his index finger from the steering wheel.

"Over there?"

"Yup."

Knowing that within the next few minutes he would get his first glimpse of Newcrest, Randall leaned back in the seat and closed his eyes.

In the darkness behind his eyelids, he tried to

foresee the possible scenarios in the same way he always did when starting a new novel. He tried to direct his inner gaze towards the ending of the story and the potential outcomes there could be.

It was a hopelessly naive thought; he knew that very well. After all, this wasn't some fictional story where the course of events could just be changed if they didn't please the great author god. This time the ending was out of his hands and there was no *Delete* button to save him. Whatever he found—or didn't find—in Newcrest would be what he had to work with.

Three possible scenarios. That was what he could boil it down to if he painted in broad strokes and didn't look at minor details.

The first scenario—and unfortunately also the least likely—was that he had been completely wrong. That there was in fact nothing wrong at all with either Allie or Billy, but that his own fears had made him read more into Allie's rejection over the phone than there actually was. It just didn't explain why her activity on social media had stopped so abruptly a little over a week ago.

The second scenario was that Allie was no longer the woman he knew. That she had become one of the blank while Billy remained the same. Randall didn't like to imagine what the boy might have been through, if that was the case. And he particularly didn't like that in this scenario there might be a chance that Billy had been kidnapped, just like David's neighbor's daughter. Or that Billy might have run away from home on his own, as David had done.

No, he would never do that. Besides, he would have called me.

His attempt to calm himself with this logic was promptly challenged by his inner version of Allie's voice:

Who says he didn't try to call you, Randall? she said. *How long do you keep your cell phone turned on each day when you're on your writer's retreat up in Maiden Lake? Five minutes? Ten?*

Of course, it wasn't difficult to shoot down that accusation, because if Billy had tried to call him, Randall would have received notifications of the missed calls when he turned on his phone.

Nevertheless, there was an element of truth in it which caused a knot of bad conscience to tie up in his belly. For had he not been so absorbed in his own world, so damned self-centered, he might have picked up the phone and called his son a little more often. And then he wouldn't be here, buried to the neck in this suffocating uncertainty.

The third scenario was the darkest. In it, both Allie and Billy had been infected with the disease and he would be left with nothing. No one to save and no happy ending.

A pull in his stomach told him that Tommy had now passed the bend and was turning onto the road that would lead them into Newcrest.

He took a deep breath and opened his eyes.

Quite rightly, their destination was straight ahead; a misty cluster of buildings of varying heights that stood in dark contrast to the light gray clouds of the overcast sky.

At the foot of the city, its skyline was mirrored in the surface of Kettle Creek, which one would have to cross via Haywood Bridge to enter Newcrest from the west.

And it was this bridge—and the four dead people hanging down from its crossbeams—that finally answered his question of whether Newcrest had escaped.

— 18 —

"If it's okay with you, I'd prefer to do it alone," Randall said when he saw his big brother move his hand down to the buckle after turning off the car's engine.

Tommy looked at him and then up at the windows of the large, red building they had parked in front of. Allie's building.

"Are you sure? What if she's ..."

He completed the sentence by running an open hand vertically up and down through the air in front of his face.

"So far, we've had no reason to believe that the blank are dangerous," Randall replied. "Besides, it's Allie we're talking about."

He didn't elaborate further, as he knew that Tommy understood what he meant. Because even though Allie was in many ways the strongest woman Randall had known in his life, it was hard to consider her a threat, physically. She was—as her father had always been able to piss her off by pointing out—a dainty, little bird.

"I'm not saying Allie is dangerous," Tommy said. "Not on her own. But should she decide to call the cops, that's another story."

"Should that happen, I'll come back to the car right away, and then we're out of here before we hear the first siren."

Tommy still wasn't crazy about the idea, that much was clear from his eyes, but after considering it for a moment, he nodded anyway. Then he turned around in the seat so he could make eye contact with David.

"What do you say, kid? You want to grab some food while he's gone?"

David raised one eyebrow, as if he wasn't quite sure whether Tommy's question was a trap. Whether he was about to fall victim to some joke he didn't understand. But when after a while Tommy still hadn't broken out in laughter, he shrugged and said:

"I am pretty hungry, but do we have any food?"

"Now, don't get all worked up," Tommy said,

winking at him. "We're talking about a couple of dry sandwiches that have been kept in a bag in the trunk all day."

David approved the menu with a raised thumb, and while he did that, Randall opened the door and stepped out.

Since the street where Allie lived was neither long nor wide—and besides ended blindly with a large wooden fence—there were rarely a lot of people to spot on it. Still, Randall was a little surprised when he looked around and discovered that he apparently had it all to himself. But then again, considering the state of the world right now, maybe that wasn't such a bad thing.

When he had gotten up the narrow concrete staircase leading up to the building's entrance, he hesitated a moment in front of the small, light gray box that served as both a doorbell for the individual apartments in the complex and a code lock for the front door.

Part of him felt he should ring the doorbell, like he used to. That he, despite the circumstances, ought to respect the privacy of his ex-wife.

Trouble was that it carried a risk. Because no matter how unlikely it seemed to him, Allie could grab the opportunity to call the police while he was on his way up the stairs to her apartment. If he, on the other hand, didn't warn her by calling first, that wouldn't be an option.

You really can't hear how crazy that sounds? How insanely paranoid you sound?

He could, and in many ways, it made him feel ashamed. But it still didn't change the fact that the fear eventually won and lead his fingers to the four numbers that unlocked the door.

Since the stairway was only illuminated by the dim gray light from outside, which could barely pass through the frosted glass plate in the door behind him, he had to feel his way over the rough wallpaper to find the light switch.

When he pushed it, a muffled, electric hum sounded, and shortly after, the room was lit up by a thin fluorescent tube hanging in the ceiling above him.

Before going up the stairs, he glanced over the mailboxes built into the wall to his left.

Twelve mailboxes, divided into two rows. Nine of the twelve were so full of envelopes and advertisements that the slots couldn't be closed completely.

He didn't like that.

Allie's was one of the nine.

He *really* didn't like that.

With increasing tension in his body, he grabbed the railing and began walking up the stairs. Under his shoes, the wood creaked treacherously with each step. Why it bothered him, he didn't quite know. But it did. So much so that he froze and grimaced every time it happened.

However, as he approached the third floor, where Allie's apartment was located, it was a new sound that stole his attention. A shrill scraping that came and went at odd intervals. It wasn't quite the sound of fingernails being dragged over a blackboard, but it was close, and it had the same spine-chilling effect on him.

With each step he took, the sound seemed to increase in strength, and when he reached the corridor on the third floor, it was clear that its origin was very close.

And Allie's door was ajar.

With a creeping sensation that something was listening just as intensely for him as he was listening for it, he forced his feet to walk the last bit over to the door.

The sound got even louder. Who or what it came from had to be somewhere in there.

He gathered his courage and pushed the door with the tip of his shoe.

The entrance hall was, like every room in Allie's apartment, decorated with a photographer's eye for balance and color combinations, and normally it would have given any visitor the feeling of having entered an open and hospitable home.

But now, when it was wrapped in a gray-blue darkness while the scraping sound relentlessly continued in the background, Randall didn't feel at home. He felt threatened.

"Allie?" he whispered, and then again, a little louder, "Are you home?"

No answer, just the damned scraping.

He continued to the end of the hallway and

stepped through the arched opening leading into the living room.

Unlike the hallway, the living room had two large windows, but the curtains were drawn and blocked off most of the daylight they would otherwise have let in. The result was that everything seemed a strange ashy gray. Even the large, colorful picture over the sofa—two hot air balloons floating in the sky over London's rooftops—seemed to have a black and white filter over it.

It was, Randall thought bitterly, as if the disease that had infected the world had also sucked all the warm colors out of it.

Reluctantly, but also with a stubborn intent to find the source of the eerie scratching sound while he could still muster the courage, he left the living room and went out into the narrow hallway that led to the kitchen. Because that was where the sound came from. He no longer had any doubts about that.

With a hand damp with sweat, he grabbed the handle of the kitchen door and pushed inwards.

As the only room in the apartment, the kitchen

was lit, and although the light source was modest—a small lamp in the hood of the stove—he had to blink a few times to get used to the light.

Her eyes were the first thing he noticed. The green eyes, which had once been a mirror to both his present and his future, but now didn't contain traces of either one. They were expressionless and stared blankly at the cupboards on the left side of the kitchen. Above and below them, blobs of yellow pus were glued to her eyelashes, and small, thin threads were drawn across the pupils each time she blinked.

The next thing Randall noticed was the plate she had in front of her on the small dining table. The plate, which made a loud screeching sound every time her hands ran the knife back and forth over it, as if she were trying to saw through an extraordinarily tough piece of meat. The same screeching sound that had led him in here.

But there was no meat on the plate. It was empty. Like the expression in her eyes.

"For Christ's sake," Randall heard himself say in a voice so thin he could barely recognize it as his own. "What are you doing, Allie? Stop that!"

Under her hands, the knife continued scratching uneven patterns in the surface of the plate's porcelain, but her face turned slightly. Not enough for him to make eye contact with her, but enough to tell him she had at least detected the sound of his voice.

"Allie," he repeated. "Allie, look at me."

Now the knife stopped, and her drowsy eyes moved a little upward, but there wasn't a shadow of recognition to be traced in them. No presence. They might as well have been made of glass.

For almost half of his life, he had woken up next to this woman—and he had never seen her like this. Hell, he wasn't sure he'd ever seen anyone like that.

A coyote. A sick coyote, driven into its last, dried-up riverbed. That was what she looked like with her messy hair, her half-open mouth, and the lumpy chunks of makeup around her eyes that looked as if it had been applied with a trowel.

He felt an urge—a very strong urge—to look away, but forced himself not to do so. Instead, he took a step closer. Then another.

"Oh God, Allie. What happened to you?"

Silence—and a soft ticking from the clock on the wall behind her—was the only answer he got.

Another step brought him close enough to be able to reach out and grab her if he wanted to. Part of him did. Part of him wanted to shake her. To *scream* at her.

But the words he wanted to scream at the top of his lungs didn't come out in a roar. They came out in a whimpering, half-suffocated whisper.

"Where is he, Allison? Where's Billy?"

No answer.

He looked over at the clock. *Tick-tock, tick-tock.* Seconds ticking by. Time he didn't have.

From the clock, his gaze slid over to the refrigerator and the photographs attached with magnets to its door. One of them was a picture of Billy.

Partly out of desperation, partly in the hope that it would make a difference, he went over and pulled it off the refrigerator door. His intention was to bring it back to the table and hold it accusingly in front of her face, as if it were a torn piece of clothing—and she the puppy who had chewed it to pieces.

But when he turned around, that plan crumbled as quickly as it had arisen in his mind, and without him being able to do anything to prevent it, the photograph slipped between his fingers and fell to the ground.

Her green eyes were still drowsy, but they no longer stared blankly into the air. They stared at him.

"Randall?" she said in a voice that sounded dry and rusty, as if it hadn't been used for a very long time. "What in God's name are you doing here?"

Really, this sudden shift shouldn't come as a big surprise for him. After all, David had described something similar when he had talked about how his mother had gradually broken down. How she at times shut down completely and was impossible to reach. Besides, Randall had also gotten a glimpse of it himself when he tried to get Joel and Kirsten to look up at the man hanging in the neon sign on the roof of Carol's Diner. Of course, it hadn't lasted as long as this, but there were a few seconds where

Joel also shut down in a similar fashion, just before he looked up from his wristwatch and said that they'd better move on.

So yes, Randall had been warned, and no, the shift shouldn't shock him. But that fact in no way made it any easier to handle. Especially now when he noticed the small wrinkles beginning to form in the forehead over Allie's hazy eyes.

Worried wrinkles. As if he was the one to be worried about.

"I ... I came to see Billy," he managed to say. It wasn't the whole truth, but it was the only part of it he was willing to give her right now. After all, he hadn't just come to see his son. He had come to pick him up.

For a long time, Allie sat motionless with a strange, pondering expression on her face. Then she suddenly blinked a few times as if she had just spotted an insect in the air close to her face and shook her head.

"I'm sorry, but Billy is not home," she said. "You should have called and let me know that you were coming. Then I could have asked him to come straight home after school."

"I did call, Allie. Last night. From Tommy's phone, remember? Where is he?"

Instead of answering, Allie got up, found a glass from one of the cupboards, and brought it over to the kitchen sink, where she turned on the cold tap and held it under the water. The entire process was carried out with stiff, almost mechanical movements, which in Randall's eyes made her look like a puppet, whose threads were controlled by the hands of an invisible puppet master.

"Where is he?" he repeated. "Where is our son, Allison?"

With the same choppy movements as before— and so slowly that he under other circumstances would have interpreted it as a deliberate provocation—Allie turned, took a sip of the water, and stared at him over the edge of the glass.

"Visiting a classmate. They had to do some group work together, I think. Biology."

"Does he have his phone with him?"

Another long hesitation and another *whoa, where did that fly come from?* blink before she nodded.

"Of course. But I'm guessing you've already tried to call him, right?"

"No, I ... I lost my phone last night, and Tommy doesn't have Billy's phone number, so I couldn't."

"So instead, you decided to drive all the way to Newcrest and show up in my kitchen unannounced? Is that how it is?"

If read in writing alone, the words that came out of her mouth would probably have seemed appropriate for a woman who was upset because her ex-husband showed up unannounced, demanding to talk to their son.

But this wasn't the dialogue of a play, and there wasn't a speck of empathy to be found in her voice. On the contrary, it sounded hollow and lifeless. As if the invisible puppet master's threads had also taken control of her vocal cords and made her reproduce something she didn't really feel—and perhaps didn't fully understand.

"I need to see him," Randall sighed, pointing to the closed blinds covering the kitchen window. "There's something very wrong with people out there, Allie, and I just want to make sure Billy's okay."

This time, the pause felt infinitely long before the answer came, and Randall started to get nervous that she was about to fall back into the same catatonic state he had found her in. But then, like an old, rusty music box whose gears suddenly got free after being stuck for a long time, she woke up with a jolt and said:

"Listen, Randall. It hasn't been very easy for Billy to make friends at his new school, so I don't intend to drag him home for no reason when he finally got an invitation. But if you're really that worried about him, you can borrow my cell phone and call him."

Although the three small words she managed to sneak into the sentence—*for no reason*—made the pulse pound a little faster in Randall's temples, he kept it in and chose not to correct her.

As cut off from reality as she was, it would lead to nothing, anyway.

"Thank you, Allie," he said instead. "I would appreciate that."

Allie responded with a mechanical nod and then

put the glass away. Then she edged past him and went out into the hallway between the living room and the kitchen, where she stopped in front of a row of clothing hooks mounted on the wall.

On one of the hooks hung a light brown handbag. After rummaging through it for a moment, she pulled out her cell phone and handed it to Randall.

He took it, hesitated a bit, and then went back to the kitchen, where he took a seat on the same chair Allie had been sitting on when he came in. He would need to sit down for this.

With trembling fingers, he turned on the screen and navigated to the phone's contact list, which he scrolled through until Billy's name appeared.

The first notes of the music started playing in almost the very second that he pressed *Call* and raised the phone to his ear. Yet it took a moment before he was able to make the connection between the two things.

But the realization came—and it was crushing.

The music was the theme of *The Mandalorian*, which was Billy's favorite series. For the same reason, it was this piece of music the boy had chosen to use as a ringtone on his phone.

And right now, that theme was playing from somewhere inside of the apartment.

— 19 —

"He must have forgotten to take it with him when he left for school this morning," Randall heard his ex-wife's sleepy voice say from the doorway behind him. "Though that doesn't sound like him."

It was an absurd conclusion to draw. Billy hadn't forgotten to bring his phone to school. Because Billy hadn't been to school—and all Randall had to do to let Allie know that was to draw her attention to the schoolbag, laying on the floor next to the boy's bedside table.

But Randall remained silent. He said nothing and didn't point at the schoolbag. He just stood there, frozen in the middle of his son's room, staring at the bed where the cell phone lay, flashing the same message on the screen at regular intervals:

MISSED CALL—MOM.

Three little, innocent words that suddenly carried an unsettling symbolism. For no matter where

Billy was and what had happened to him, one thing had become very clear to Randall over the last half hour:

Billy no longer had a mother who was able to take care of him. That responsibility had to fall solely on him now—whether he felt qualified or not.

It was a harsh realization. But also, a necessary realization—and it was what finally enabled Randall to break free from the shock and focus on the task at hand.

He had to take care of his son—and to do that, he would have to find him first. This meant that the anxiety, the panic, and all the other emotions that threatened to drag him down into the abyss had to be pushed into the background.

With that thought as the driving force, he went over to the bed, picked up the cell phone, and ran his thumb sideways across the screen, so the blinking message disappeared. Then he put the phone in his pocket and turned towards Allie.

"I'm taking his phone with me," he said. "Maybe there's something on it that can help me to figure out where he is."

"I've already told you that ..." Allie began, but Randall stopped her by raising his hand.

"And I will find him," he added, more to himself than to her. "That I promise."

The words weighed heavily and burned his throat as he uttered them. But to Allie in the doorway, they made no noticeable impression. She just stared absently at him for a moment and then shrugged.

"Are you sure you don't want to just wait here until he comes home?" she asked. "I could make some coffee, and then you could tell me all about the new book while we wait."

Despite her distant look and toneless voice, Randall had to bite his lip to hold back the tears. Twenty-four hours ago, there was nothing in the world he would rather have done. Sitting on the couch, chatting about his books and her photos over a cup of coffee was one of the things he missed most from their old life.

And it was, truth be told, also part of the dream scenario he had envisioned when he had written the last sentence in his new book. The scenario in which he saw himself sitting on the edge of the bed behind him right now, reading aloud to his son— and where Billy would slowly but surely realize that THE LONGEST WAY was in fact about them.

"Unfortunately, I can't stay here, Allie," he said, sighing. "Tommy is in the car waiting for me."

Allie tilted her head slightly and stared at nothing for a moment. Then the invisible puppet master pulled at the threads connected to the corners of her mouth and forced her lips up into a smile. One that was so fake that Randall had to look away.

"Oh well," she said. "I'll make sure to tell Billy you came by and get him to call you. Say hello to Tommy from me, okay?"

"I ... I will make sure to do that," Randall said, but even before he had gotten all the way through the sentence, Allie had lost interest and disappeared out of sight behind the door frame.

He considered following her. Giving it one last try. But his feet refused to move, and he ended up just standing there.

When a while later he heard her pull the chair

out from the table in the kitchen—and when, after another pause, he heard her resume the impossible project of filleting a piece of meat that had never been there—he didn't go out to her either.

Instead, he made the heavy but inevitable decision and left the room—and then the apartment—in silence and with a heavy heart.

Out by the stairs in the hallway, the light had gone out again, but he didn't turn it on right away. For though the darkness still was a little intimidating, he also found something strangely soothing in it.

Maybe because in the dark he didn't feel he needed to hide the tears starting to flow down his cheeks.

When there were no more tears left, he wiped his cheeks, took as deep a breath as his lungs could handle, and let the air out again.

Better. A little better.

He turned on the light, grabbed the railing, and hurried down the stairs. He felt he had to. On the one hand, he was afraid that he would suffer another, perhaps bigger breakdown if he stopped, and on the other hand, he simply needed to get out. Out on the street, where he could breathe freely—and where he could no longer hear Allie scraping that fucking knife against the surface of the plate.

Outside, he was met by the sound of Tommy and David's voices. They were still sitting in the car with the window rolled down on one side. What the subject of their conversation was, he was still too far away to decide, but it didn't sound like anything particularly heavy. On the whole, the mood seemed to be somewhat more uplifted than it had been half an hour ago when he got out of the car.

That didn't last long, however, because as soon as Tommy caught sight of him, his smile was replaced with a serious expression. One which promptly spread to David's face as well.

"So," Tommy said, as Randall opened the door and let himself fall down in the passenger seat. "Did you talk to the bumblebee? Is he okay?"

Randall shook his head and sighed.

"He wasn't there. Allie was home, but not Billy."

"Did she say where he was?"

Randall let out a grunt of despair and shook his

head once more.

"She claimed he went straight home to a friend's after school."

Although Tommy caught himself in the act and tried to hide it, Randall saw his eyes turn to the sky.

"It was bad up there, Tommy," Randall continued. "Billy's phone was on the bed, and his schoolbag was on the floor in his room. Still, Allie was convinced he had been to school and that he was at a friend's house now. She is ..."

"She is what?"

"She ... she's not herself anymore, Tommy. She is completely lost in her own world."

"Like my mom," David said bitterly in the back seat.

Randall caught his gaze in the side mirror and nodded. Then he turned back to Tommy.

"Allie is one of them now, one of the blank. I couldn't get through to her at all, and ... and to be completely honest, I'm not sure I ever will be able to."

Tommy looked at him, *studied* him, for a long time.

"I'm sorry," he then said. "What the hell do we do now?"

Despite the state of confusion and powerlessness he felt trapped in right now, that particular question was one Randall didn't have to think about for long. In fact, it was probably the only thing remaining that he had a clear answer to.

"Find Billy," he said. "That's what we do now. We find out where Billy is. And when we've done that, we bring him home."

— 20 —

Randall got none of what he had hoped to achieve by taking Billy's cell phone with him. It told him neither where the boy was nor what had happened to him. The only thing it did was confirm that Billy had probably been missing for almost an entire week. At least something significant had happened six days ago. Because that was when the boy had suddenly stopped replying to his messages.

The last message he had sent out was to Allie: An animated picture of Patrick—the big, pink starfish from *SpongeBob SquarePants*—who was in the process of emptying an entire dish of burgers down his throat, followed by the text: *What are we having for dinner?*

The message hadn't been answered, and though Randall knew he was just tormenting himself, he couldn't help but wonder what it might mean. Had Allie already changed by that time? And if so, was Billy a witness to her change? Had he been standing on the sidelines, watching helplessly as his mother gradually disintegrated and became the ... thing that was sitting in the apartment now, feverishly chopping away at an empty plate?

No. The pieces simply didn't fit together. If that was the case, Billy would have sought help, either from him or others close to him. And there was no sign that he had done so. Which meant that Billy ...

"Randall, are you listening?"

The sound of Tommy's voice made Randall jump and the cell phone in his hands almost ended up on the floor.

"Sorry, Tommy. I ... I'm just a bit shaken."

"And that's no fucking wonder," Tommy said. "But you need to tell us what you want us to do. We can't just sit here all day."

Here was the street outside Allie's apartment, where they were still parked. And Tommy was right. They achieved nothing by staying here. The only problem was that Randall had no useful answer to that question and it was driving him insane.

"I know, Tommy," he replied. "I know, damn it. I

just need to think, okay?"

He was aware of the anger in his voice, and he was also aware that it was unfair to direct it at Tommy. Yet he did nothing to hold it back. He desired a confrontation, an argument ... anything that could give him an outlet for his desperation and despair.

But Tommy didn't bite. He just looked at him and shook his head slowly from side to side.

"There is no reason for you to bark. It isn't fair, not to me, not to the kid, and you know it."

"Not fair? My son has gone missing and you're talking about what's fair?"

"I know Billy's gone, and I understand how hard it must be, but ..."

"But do you know, Tommy?" Randall said—and now it was actually starting to feel as if the anger indeed was directed to the right place. "Do you really *understand* it?"

The words—the symbolic fishing hook, which he now for the third time let dangle before the nose of his brother in the hope of starting a fight—were allowed to hang in the air for a few seconds while the wrinkles drew waves and webs across Tommy's face.

And then he finally took the bait.

"What the hell is that supposed to mean?"

Knowing that it would be the most efficient lighter fluid if he wanted to turn the small, smoldering embers in Tommy's eyes into a blazing fire, Randall replied with a shrug.

"That I don't have children and therefore cannot possibly comprehend the pain you feel?" Tommy continued. "Is that it?"

"Something like that."

"You know what? Fuck you, Randall. *Fuck* you! I should have hung up when you called and left you in that parking lot."

"Maybe," Randall said, looking up at the windows of Allie's building. "It doesn't seem like it made much of a difference, does it?"

In the back seat, David moved uneasily from side to side, clearly anxious about the situation, but neither Randall nor his brother took notice of it.

"So what?" replied Tommy. "Now you're just gonna throw in the towel and give up?"

"I don't know. You tell me. You're the expert in that field."

The last sentence crossed the line, by far, but before Randall realized that, the words had already left his mouth.

"I knew it," Tommy hissed between clenched teeth. "No matter what I say or do, that's always where it's gonna end, right? Tommy, the sloppy drug addict who was never anything but a disappointment to his family. The loser, who couldn't even be bothered to take care of his poor old father when he became ill."

"That is not what I meant," Randall tried, but Tommy wasn't done—and let him know it by beating his open hand against the steering wheel.

"Yes, it was, Randall. That was *exactly* what you meant. Why else is it that we haven't talked to each other since the funeral?"

He paused for a moment and waved his hand as if to say: *If you have a better answer, then feel free to speak up.*

Randall didn't have an answer. At least not one he could spit out on command from the corner he had been pushed into.

"You turned your back on me, Randall, and you weren't the only one. Hell, with the exception of Mom, our whole family turned their backs on me. And for what? Because you didn't like to hear the truth. But you know what? I told you then, I told you last night, and I will tell you now: I still stand by it. Why should I take care of Dad when he was never there when I needed him?"

"For Mom's sake," Randall said bitterly. "You could have swallowed your pride for her sake. Or you could have just stayed away from the funeral. You didn't have to show up."

And you definitely didn't have to get wasted and give a long speech would have been the next words if Randall hadn't noticed the sudden shift in Tommy's face. But he did notice. He saw it stiffen, saw the anger turn to shame, and it gave him a stab of bad conscience.

"Now, listen," he said instead. "I'm not saying he was the best dad in the world. We both know he wasn't. But Mom loved him, and ... and instead of allowing her to give him the funeral she wanted,

222

you went and made it about you."

Tommy fished a cigarette out of his pocket and turned his face away as he lit it. Like that he remained—silent and with his gaze fixated on his own reflection in the side window—for what felt like an eternity, before he turned around again and met his brother's gaze.

"Actually, I visited him once while he was in the hospital," he said. "Did he ever tell you that?"

Randall shook his head and Tommy shrugged.

"Oh well, but I did. Mom had asked me to several times, so eventually I went there."

He paused briefly while tapping the cigarette against the edge of the half-open window, so small pieces of ash sprinkled off it and fell out onto the road.

"It was pretty awkward, and I don't remember most of what we talked about. But there is one thing that I remember very clearly."

He took a drag of the cigarette, held the smoke in for a few seconds, and then let it out in a long sigh.

"Back then, I had just received a badge from the

AA group. Two years with no relapse. Not even one crappy beer. I was so fucking proud of it, I tell you. And do you know what our dear father said when I showed it to him?"

Randall shook his head.

"One more for the collection," Tommy sighed. "That was it. He stared at it for a few seconds and then handed it back to me with those words. One more for the collection."

It would be a lie if Randall claimed he was surprised. Richard Morgan wasn't exactly known for being a man who pulled on the velvet gloves and wrapped things nicely before serving them. And at some point along the way he had indeed given up on Tommy. That was no secret either. But from there and then to trample his own son down so cynically, just as he was getting up ... that was something.

For a while, Randall sat in silence with his gaze fixed on his hands as he digested what Tommy had told him. He was looking for something nice to say, found nothing, and ended up putting a hand on his brother's shoulder instead.

Tommy let him do it. Because the fight was over now, and they both knew it.

When a bit later he had let go of Tommy's shoulder, Randall looked to the back seat to see if David, who had been an involuntary witness to the argument, was okay.

David didn't look okay. In fact, he looked as if he had just seen a ghost marching by on the sidewalk outside.

"Sorry about that, David," Randall said. "The waves tend to roll a bit high sometimes when Tommy and I are together."

The sound of his own name made David look up, but it still seemed as if his thoughts were far away. Then he blinked.

"What? No, it wasn't that. I just remembered something when Tommy said that stuff about your dad at the hospital. I ... I can't believe I'm only seeing it now, but I think I may have an idea as to how we can find your son."

He narrowed his eyes for a moment and then nodded.

"My dad was a doctor. I don't think I told you

that before, but he was. And I think that's why he didn't become like my mom when he changed. I think what got him sick and made him drive away with Emma also affected many of the doctors and nurses he worked with. At least there was something wrong at the hospital. He told me that several weeks ago. Back when he was still well."

"Wrong how?"

"At first, he just complained that he didn't think the others were doing their job properly," David said, shrugging. "He said they rejected a whole lot of patients for no reason. People who needed treatment. But at the end, just before he himself changed, he said it was as if they were deliberately trying to empty out the hospital."

"For what purpose?" Randall asked, even though he already knew the answer. At least he feared he did.

"Well, I can't be sure," David replied. "But I think maybe they were getting ready for ... you know, something with the kids."

Randall turned to Tommy, who immediately raised his hand to show that he had already grabbed the cell phone.

After entering the search words, he turned it towards Randall so he could follow along on the screen.

The map started off by showing the whole of Pennsylvania and fragments of the surrounding states. Then it zoomed in on Newcrest—and then on the red spot that marked the most relevant search result for the word that Tommy had entered.

NEWCREST MEMORIAL HOSPITAL.

Randall read the words and then exchanged a glance, first with Tommy, then with David.

None of them hesitated to nod.

— 21 —

Even before he opened the car door and set foot on the asphalt in the empty parking lot in front of Newcrest Memorial Hospital, there was something that gave Randall the feeling—no, the *conviction*—that not everything was as it should be within the hospital walls. And when he got out of the car, that feeling only got stronger.

Part of the explanation was obvious, because even though there was light behind the glass doors at the entrance and in a large part of the windows, there were no people to be seen inside.

But that was only part of the explanation, as it was not only behind the windows that there were no people in sight. The parking lot and the entire surrounding area were also devoid of life. And what was perhaps even more telling: It was devoid of *death*, which stood in sharp contrast to what they had experienced on the way here, where Newcrest had offered far more hangings than the other towns. But not a single person had been hanged here—and this despite the fact that there was almost the same number of lampposts as there were parking bays in each row.

"I'm bringing the rifle, just in case," Tommy whispered. He was the first one out of the car and was now standing with his head buried in the trunk. "Is there anything else you want to bring?"

"Did you eat all the sandwiches?"

Tommy popped his head out over the top of the tailgate and sent Randall a look that clearly meant something along the lines of: *Seriously? What do you take us for?*

"*Of course*, we saved one for you. Anything else? I see that you put the folder with your book manuscript in the bag. Do you want to bring it? Imagine if someone were to steal it while we were away and take credit for your genius."

"A sandwich will do," Randall said with as light and carefree a tone of voice as he was able to muster. He both recognized and appreciated that Tommy was trying to lighten the tense mood with a witty comment.

Besides, if he was being honest, he wasn't too keen on letting his big brother know that he actually wasn't happy about leaving the manuscript in the trunk.

Tommy nodded and then disappeared back down behind the trunk lid. Meanwhile, Randall walked over to David, who was standing on the other side of the car with his hands in his pockets. The hood of his sweatshirt was pulled so far down over his forehead that it covered most of his hair, but his eyes were still visible. They were directed towards the entrance to the hospital—and the expression in them carried a clear message.

"You don't have to come along, you know. You can just stay here."

David gave him a frozen smile and shrugged.

"It's okay. I don't mind."

"Okay. As long as it's not because you feel you owe us something. Because you don't."

"I'd be hanging in a lamppost in Ridgeview right now if it weren't for you guys. I'm going."

His tone of voice didn't invite a debate, and Randall decided to respect that. Therefore, he simply nodded.

Behind them, the car's tailgate was slammed shut with a bang that made them both jerk.

"Christ, Tommy. Was it really necessary to do it so hard?"

"My bad," Tommy said, raising his hands apologetically. "It just slipped. Are we ... are we ready?"

Randall and David exchanged a glance and nodded. Then the three of them began to walk over to the large glass doors at the entrance to the hospital.

As they walked, a nagging thought emerged in Randall's mind: What if it wasn't a coincidence that all these lampposts had gone free? What if someone—or some*thing*—told the police to stay away from here? That it was forbidden territory.

"What the hell?"

The surprised outburst made him look up, first at Tommy, where it had come from, then at the spot where both Tommy and David's wide-open eyes were looking.

What—with good reason—had caught their attention was the tin roof, which was mounted on the outer wall on the right side of the hospital entrance to provide shelter for bicycles and other two-wheeled vehicles.

There just wasn't a lot of shelter to be found in the bike shed right now, as two of the roof's plates had been ripped apart and now hung limply down on either side.

Beneath them was a hole in the asphalt—and at its center was the strange object that must have caused the destruction.

"What the hell is that?" Tommy groaned in a voice so shrill it made him sound like a child. "A missile? Seriously? That's their solution? To have the military drop a bomb and blow the shit up?"

It wasn't difficult to see why this was Tommy's first thought, as the projectile did have some of the characteristics that one would associate with a military missile—tear shape, steering fins, and so on. Yet Randall instinctively knew that this wasn't the right explanation.

Because this wasn't something the military was behind. Firstly, there were no letters, numbers, or other identifying symbols on the thing, and secondly, the dark gray material it was made of was unlike anything he had ever seen before. It looked like some kind of metal, but something about the structure made the surface seem ... *unsteady*. As if it had been coated with a wet paint that was constantly in motion but just wasn't subject to the laws of physics and therefore flowed in all directions. Including directions that gravity should have made impossible.

So no, the military wasn't responsible for this. No military they knew of, at least. This came from somewhere else.

He turned around to present this logic to Tommy—and immediately read in his face that it wasn't necessary. The penny had dropped, hard and heavy, on him now.

"We joked about it, Randall," he groaned, rubbing both hands over his cheeks. "We made fun of it, and now ..."

Randall heard the despair in his brother's voice, and for a moment he was on the verge of giving in to it himself. Then he took a deep breath, clasped his hands and—quite literally—shook the feeling off.

"I know," he said. "But beating ourselves up about it now won't help us. And it won't help Billy either if he's actually in there. We'll have to keep our heads cool, okay?"

Tommy nodded, let out a long, strained sigh, and then nodded again.

"We go in, find Billy—and then we get the fuck away from this creepy hospital. Deal?"

"Deal."

— 22 —

According to the inscription in the bronze plaque on the stone sculpture by the small indoor fountain, it was only six years ago that Newcrest Memorial Hospital had been built. Yet, it felt as if they had entered a museum or an old library when they crossed the threshold of the large room that functioned—or rather *had* functioned—as the hospital's entrance hall.

It had to be the silence. The deep, ominous silence that amplified the sound of their own footsteps and at the same time filled them with the feeling that any type of noise would have consequences in this place.

"What's the plan?" David whispered. "And don't suggest some horror movie shit, where we split up and get slaughtered one by one."

Randall gave him a crooked smile and then raised his hand as a signal that he needed a moment to think.

The left side of the entrance hall, he could quickly cross off the list, as it was dedicated to the cafeteria and the gift shop. The right side wasn't very interesting either. The only thing it offered was the door out to a covered walkway, which cut through a green area outside and ended at a pavilion with benches and tables.

Remaining was the middle section of the entrance hall, from which one could enter the two central corridors that served as links to the medical departments. One was accessible from where they stood, but to get to the other, one had to take an escalator—which didn't seem to have been running for a good while.

And that was what Randall ended up pointing to.

"I suggest we start from the top and move downwards," he said. "How does that sound?"

Tommy and David both approved the proposal, one with a raised thumb, the other with a nod, after which they turned around and began walking towards the escalator.

Traversing its steps was surprisingly hard, and

when they reached the first floor, they paused for a moment to catch their breath.

And—truth be told—to gather the courage to enter the long, empty corridor that stretched out in front of them.

"I knew it," David sighed, shaking his head. "I just knew it would be like this."

He didn't elaborate and didn't need to. Randall perfectly understood what he was referring to. And he also didn't doubt that Tommy did as well.

It was the fluorescent tube. The one that stuck out among the many because it was nearing the end of its lifespan and let the world know it by flashing unsteadily.

This could easily have been the backdrop for a horror movie, Randall thought. But what he chose to say out loud was:

"Yeah, whatever, it's just a lamp. Let's just keep going."

"Maybe we should take a look at that first," Tommy said, pointing to a large sign that hung on the wall some distance inside the corridor. "I think there's a map in the corner of it."

There *was* a map. Not of the entire hospital, but of the floor they were on. The left side was a drawn overview. On it, the various departments were indicated with number and letter abbreviations, which could be decoded using a list of the departments' full names on the right side.

As he read them, Randall followed the lines with his finger—and when he reached the penultimate line of the list, that finger began to tremble.

B7: PEDIATRIC WARD/BED SECTION.

He felt something touch his shoulder, turned around and was greeted by Tommy's gray eyes. They looked worried.

"I'm okay. It all just became very real all of a sudden, you know."

Tommy said nothing but simply put his hand on Randall's shoulder and gently led him forward.

With the exception of the spooky fluorescent tube that kept turning on and off in an unpredictable pattern, the long corridor was bathed in light. Still, Randall couldn't see all the way down to the end.

Infinite. That was how it seemed to him. So did

the number of doors and adjoining sidewalks that they would need to examine.

The first door they came to was locked. The next two were open, but revealed nothing but empty, darkened bed sections.

The third door led into a guard room. Here there was light, but that in no way made it less scary than the dark bed sections. Because even though the guard room was empty right now, it looked as if it had been manned not long ago. The computer on the desk was turned on, and next to it was a telephone with the handset taken off, emitting a faint dial tone. A bit further to the right, a folder with a patient record lay open under a lit desk lamp.

Maybe the hospital wasn't as empty as it seemed. Then the question was whether that was good or bad news.

After passing another couple of empty rooms with empty beds, they came to the central corridor's first crossing. Both branches were closed off behind large, semi-automatic double doors, and as they pulled on the cord which opened the doors to the left, the three of them instinctively took a step back.

The hallway behind the door was a chaotic mess. All sorts of medical devices stood along the walls, set aside, as if there had been no space left for them in the storage rooms. Large, massive machines with plastic hoses hanging down from them like tentacles.

Still, there were no people in sight, neither hospital staff nor missing children. Not in the hallway itself nor in any of the rooms it gave access to. Empty beds, empty toilets, and empty offices. That was all.

With rising discouragement in their hearts, they returned to the main aisle and continued their search of the first floor.

Hallway after hallway, door after door, they drove on, with the same fruitless result, until they finally stood in front of a double door, on which the words Randall had dreaded to see ever since he read them on the map earlier were written.

B7: PEDIATRIC WARD/BED SECTION.

— 23 —

The three empty beds, where crumpled duvets and sheets hung down over the edge in a crooked angle, as if the patients had tried to cling to them while they were being pulled out of bed against their will. The trolley, crammed to the brim with dirty bed linen that was soaked in yellowish liquid and stank to high heaven. The teddy bears randomly scattered across the floor, as if they had been kicked around for fun.

These things—and countless others in Section B7—could have done it. But it was the drawing that delivered the killing blow and made the pulse beat so hard in Randall's temples that it whistled and clicked in his ears.

The drawing hung among several others on a notice board next to a bookcase with toys on the right side of the room. A completely ordinary piece of paper with a completely ordinary subject that wouldn't surprise anyone visiting the pediatric ward of a hospital.

It wasn't even a particularly good drawing. The wings were out of proportion, and at one of the stripes, the artist—according to the signature in the lower left corner, a seven-year-old boy named MARCUS—had clearly colored a little too far beyond the lines by accident.

But the intention was clear enough. Any spectator would instantly be able to see that it was supposed to represent a bumblebee.

In an attempt to stop the thoughts he knew were coming, Randall put his hands over his eyes and pressed until small, silvery lightning bolts began to shoot forth in the darkness behind his closed eyelids.

But it was in vain. The officer stepped out of that very same darkness and spread his arms out to the sides, as he had done in the pouring rain on Highway 55, where he uttered the words that weren't meant for his mouth.

For my son, Billy. My little bumblebee.

Randall pressed harder. The officer disappeared, but his place was taken by Allie, who was sitting at the kitchen table sawing at the plate while Billy was dragged out of the apartment, kicking and screaming.

The sound of a sharp crack close to Randall's face tore the image apart and made him open his eyes. It was Tommy who had snapped his fingers right in front of him.

"We have to move away from the doorway," he whispered. "Somebody's coming."

For a few seconds, Randall wasn't able to understand what Tommy was trying to tell him. Then he heard it too.

Footsteps echoing along with the faint rustle of a bundle of keys. Whistling wheels being pulled over a tiled floor.

As quickly and silently as he could, he joined David and Tommy, who had gone into hiding behind the open door.

Part of him felt a strong urge to look out through the small window in the middle of the door, but he resisted it and kept his head low as the footsteps slowly rose in volume and then fell again as the porter passed the entrance to B7.

Because it was a porter. A porter pushing a hospital bed in front of him. The shadow had told him as much as it slid past on the floor between the doors.

Without warning—and so abruptly that it couldn't be because the man had moved out of earshot—the sounds suddenly stopped.

Randall exchanged a worried look with David and Tommy, who both asked him the same wordless question by raising their hands, palms up.

Why did he stop? Did he hear us?

The answer came. Not from Randall's mouth, but from somewhere out in the corridor. The sound of a bell, followed by a muffled rumble.

Elevator doors sliding open.

An idea—concrete and intrusive—shot down into Randall's head. He listened, waited, and as soon as he heard the doors of the elevator close, he jumped out of his hiding place and ran out into the hallway.

"What are you doing?"

Tommy's voice sounded tense, on the verge of panic, but Randall didn't have time to worry about that. He didn't know if the number would disappear or remain on the display when the elevator reached its stop, so he couldn't waste time on long explanations.

And that was a good decision, because the red lines that together formed a digital four on the small, black screen above the elevator doors disappeared the moment he got there.

But he got a glimpse of them. He managed to see where the first human being they had seen at Newcrest Memorial so far had gotten off.

And he intended to follow.

— 24 —

The porter turned out to be a PARAMEDIC. At least
that was what was written in capital letters on the
back of his reflective safety vest.

However, keeping up and keeping distance at
the same time was no easier for that reason, and it
didn't take long before they completely lost sight of
him in the large, white maze.

Luckily, it wasn't the end of the world, because
by that time they had already found something else
to navigate by. Via a long, floating walkway with
large glass windows, which had a view down to the
green area Randall had seen from the entrance hall
earlier, the fourth floor in this building was connected to one of the hospital's other parts. And
somewhere at the end of that walkway, the distant
clanking of equipment revealed the existence of
other people.

"Is there something wrong?" Randall asked
when they had gotten a few feet out on the walk-

way, and he discovered David had started to fall behind.

It was a rhetorical question, for the pale color of the teenager's face gave a clear hint as to what had stopped him.

"I ... I'm not too fond of heights," David said, smiling embarrassedly.

"Just don't look down."

David answered Tommy's advice with a look that didn't hide how much he thought it was worth.

"Gee, thanks, I hadn't considered that at all."

"Just trying to be helpful," Tommy said, shrugging.

"By the way, I've been meaning to ask you," Randall said. "Did you do graffiti? Before all this, I mean."

David stared at him for a moment and then shook his head.

"No, there were a couple from my class who did, but they weren't exactly in the group I hung out with. Also, it's illegal in most places, and ... I don't know. It just isn't me."

"So what did you do when you were with your

friends? You must have had some kind of hobby, right?"

David shrugged.

"We played a lot online."

"Yeah, of course," Randall said, nodding. "Billy was the same. You'd think you'd have to pry his cold dead fingers off the Playstation once Fortnite was launched. Do you know that game?"

"Yeah, we played that too sometimes. But mostly it was Call of Duty."

"And what about the big question?"

"What do you mean?"

"Console or computer?"

"Computer, of course. No comparison."

"Fair enough."

What Randall was trying to do was obvious—no doubt to the recipient as well—but it worked as intended. His questions diverted David's attention from the windows and enabled him to move his feet.

Slowly but surely, they reached the opposite side of the bridge, where they were met by another semi-automatic double door, which could be opened by pulling on a string that hung from the ceiling.

This time, however, they didn't use the string. Instead, Tommy put his shoulder against one of the doors and pushed until he had created a crack he could look through.

"It's just like on the other side," he whispered. "A long aisle with lots of doors. It looks like it's clear, but we need to be more careful over here. There is definitely staffing in this building."

He froze and then slowly pulled his head back from the crack.

"There's someone out there," he said so quietly that it was barely audible. "Two doctors, I think. They're wearing coats."

"Are they coming this way?"

Tommy took another look through the crack. Then he shook his head.

"Right now, they're just standing there, talking, but ... no, wait. I think they're leaving."

He hesitated for a few seconds and then nodded.

"Yup, they're leaving. And they're going the right way."

"So the coast is clear?"

Tommy answered the question by easing up the door and stepping out into the hallway—and as it didn't trigger neither alarms nor terrifying war cries, Randall and David followed.

Although the main corridor of this building was confusingly similar to the one they had trotted through on the other side, it somehow felt way more intimidating.

The muffled voices and the occasional rattle of equipment in the background—and in general, the awareness that they were no longer alone—were of course part of the reason. But there was something else as well.

Maybe it was just the simple feeling that they now had gotten their *where*, but still lacked their *what*.

With this thought gnawing in the back of his head, Randall pulled on his leader's cap and signaled the others to follow him down to a crossing in the main aisle. From there, he turned left and led them into one of the smaller, adjacent hallways. He saw no reason for them to be parading around out in the large corridor, where anyone would be able to see them coming a mile away.

"Obs. room, stud.," Tommy read aloud from a sign hanging on one of the hallway's doors. "What does that mean?"

"It's for the medical students," David explained. "So they can see how an operation is performed. There is probably an operating room downstairs, and then they can follow along from some windows up here. That way they don't disturb the surgeons."

Tommy raised one eyebrow and sent him a nod of approval.

"My ... my dad showed it to me once," David elaborated. "Sometimes he also had an *audience*, as he called it."

The hallway ended in another door, which led them into a narrow storage room, where the walls were covered with long shelves filled with bed linen and lab coats as well as cardboard boxes with hair nets, masks, rubber gloves, and similar hospital equipment.

To get to the door at the opposite end of the room, they had to edge past another cart with dirty bedding and a wheelchair that someone had left in the middle of the narrow passageway between the shelves.

As they did so, Randall saw out of the corner of his eye that David had pulled the top of his hoodie up, so it covered his mouth and nose. He was just about to ask about it when the answer hit his own nostrils. A stale, moist smell of urine and worn-out fabric.

It really shouldn't smell like that, he thought as he followed David's example and pulled his own shirt up in front of his mouth. *Not in a hospital.*

When they had advanced a bit further, however, it was the incoming signal from one of his other four senses that caught his attention.

At first his ears claimed that it was coming from the vent in the ceiling above them, but as they approached the door, he started to doubt it. Because the strange noise could also be coming from somewhere out there.

Radio noise?

No, he didn't think so. It was close, but there was a wavy, almost melodic movement in the pitch of this sound that one wouldn't find in static radio noise.

Unlike the door they came from, the door at the other end of the storage room had a small, built-in windowpane that they could use to check if there was a clear path on the other side.

There was ... sort of. Because even though there were no people to be seen, the long corridor on the other side of the glass had an obvious problem. There were no adjoining hallways to seek cover in if they should encounter traffic. In fact, the only potential hiding places were two doors, which according to the signs led into the same *AUDITORIUM*. And both doors they would have to walk a good distance across the open corridor to reach.

"It's too open," Tommy whispered. "You'll have to wait here while I slip over and check if it's safe."

Before the sentence was even finished, David began to shake his head.

"That wasn't the deal," he said. "The deal was that we were *not* going to do some horror movie shit where we split up."

"Listen, kid," Tommy said, patiently as a teacher

working with a slow student. "If the door is locked over there, we are screwed. And then it wouldn't be too bright to have three people prancing around over there if one is enough. Do you see what I mean?"

David stared defiantly at him for a moment. When it produced no useful result, he turned his gaze to Randall, asking for support.

Though he would have liked to, Randall couldn't present a better plan than the one Tommy had thrown on the table, and he let the young man know it by shaking his head. Then he turned to his brother.

"If it's locked, you'll come straight back here."

Tommy nodded.

"I mean it, Tommy. No funny business and no improvisation. If it's open, you give us a sign and we'll come running. But if the door is locked, you get your ass back here right away."

Tommy nodded again. He wasn't quite able to stifle the smile that had begun to form in the corners of his mouth, but he made the attempt, and that was at least something.

"Good," Randall said. "Now, fuck off."

Tommy topped off his last nod with a two-fingered salute, after which he turned around and glanced out the window before pushing the door open.

From the same window, Randall and David followed him with their eyes as he tiptoed across the floor of the corridor.

Once he had safely reached the door to the *AUDITORIUM*, Tommy—slowly and cautiously—grabbed the handle and pulled. The door followed his hand backward, and he sent them a smile and a raised thumb.

After opening the door a little more, he leaned his head in towards the frame and looked in through the opening.

For a while he stood like that. A *long* while. And then, instead of fully opening the door and entering, he suddenly let go of the handle and began to—quite literally—back away from it.

That way, staggering backward with stiff, jagged steps, he continued backward until he had covered almost half the distance he had walked to get there.

"What happened?" David asked. "What the hell did he see in there?"

"I don't know, but it ..."

The sentence was never completed, because just then Tommy turned around—and the sight of his pale face made Randall's vocal cords tighten up.

"I'm going out to him."

David took a deep breath as if he was about to protest, but then let it out in a frustrated sigh.

"Just be quick, okay?"

"I will."

With those words, Randall pushed open the door and ran out to his brother, who was still frozen in the same spot in the middle of the long corridor.

"It's the kids," Tommy said when there was only three feet of distance left between them. "I found them. Oh God, Randall. They ..."

He said something more, but at that point Randall had already pushed past him.

— 25 —

From the humming video projector in the ceiling and down to the stage at the end of the sloping rows of chairs, the auditorium stretched across at least three of the building's floors, making it by far the largest room Randall had seen at Newcrest Memorial Hospital.

Nonetheless, the room at first glance filled him with a sense of claustrophobia that was stronger and more intrusive than anything he had ever experienced before. It grabbed him, enveloped him like a straitjacket made from concrete, and squeezed until it felt as if his lungs would explode in his chest.

It was no wonder Tommy was pale as a corpse when he came back from here. No fucking wonder.

As they sat there on the rows of chairs, illuminated only by the faint, flickering reflection of the film up on the canvas, they hardly looked real. Had it not been for the faint movement of their chests when they breathed in and out, they could just as well have been wax figures.

But it wasn't wax figures populating the seats in the semi-darkness of the auditorium. It was children. Small, pale children sitting shoulder to shoulder in endless rows, all with their eyes fixed on the incoherent stream of images the projector threw up on the screen.

Nothing about the flickering images made sense to Randall, but he also didn't make any effort to understand it. His full attention was focused on the poles with IV bags that were lined up behind the seats in every single row of chairs—and that drop by drop sent some silvery liquid into the children's veins.

Mercury? No, that would be way too thick for those thin plastic hoses ... wouldn't it?

The nearest drop stand was no more than a few feet away. Yet he had to force a deep breath all the way down to the bottom of his lungs before he was able to walk over to it.

With fingers where all feeling seemed to have disappeared, he grabbed the corner of the drop bag and turned it slowly from side to side while studying the contents.

The liquid splashed, faster than mercury would have done, up and down the sides of the bag, but he didn't know if he should feel relieved or not. Because even though it was very toxic, you at least knew what mercury was. This foreign liquid could very well turn out to be ten times ...

A gasp escaped his lips, and his fingers let go of the bag, as if it were a piece of burning coal.

Something had moved in there. Something *living* had fucking moved inside the bag.

He could see them now. No matter how little he wanted to, he could see them swimming around in there. Tiny shadows that occasionally touched the plastic so you could see their disgusting little curvy tails.

Reluctantly, his gaze followed, as one of the shadows slid down through the thin plastic hose and then disappeared into the arm of the little girl who was sitting motionless on the seat in front of him.

In shock he stared at her face, waiting for the

reaction that ought to come, but never did. Not even a small pull in the corners of the mouth or a twitch of the hand. The girl just kept staring absently up at the canvas with eyes that never seemed to blink while this disgusting foreign organism invaded her bloodstream.

As she did when Randall grabbed her shoulder and shook it—first gently, then gradually harder.

Neither led to an abrupt awakening—not for the girl at least. As for himself, however, there was an awakening of a kind. Because somewhere, deep down in his subconscious, there was a locked door, which was now ripped off its hinges. And what waited on the other side was a realization that was so unbearable and shameful that it forced him to his knees.

"Tommy?"

"I'm here," sounded behind him.

"It's too much. I can't, I ... I'm not strong enough."

"Of course, you are, Randall. Stop saying that bullshit and get up."

Tommy's voice was hard and unwavering, but

the touch of his hand, as he placed it on Randall's shoulder, was gentle and soft. Almost unnoticeable.

"Get up," he repeated. "We are so close now. This is the finish line, damn it. For all we know, Billy is sitting somewhere down there right now waiting for us. So, man up, Randall. Man up and get up."

Just as gently as it had been put there, Randall felt Tommy's hand pull away from his shoulder. A second later, it appeared on the edge of his field of vision.

There it stayed, patiently waiting in the air to the left of his face, until he had gained enough control over his emotions to take it and let himself be pulled up.

"Sorry," he said when he was back on his feet. "I ... I don't know what got into me."

"Forget about it," Tommy replied, patting him on the back. "You would have to be a pretty cold shit not to let this affect you. Now let's go find Billy, okay?"

Randall nodded, and Tommy turned his attention to David, who was still standing in the doorway.

"We'll need someone to keep watch while we're looking. Are you the man for that, kid?"

For a moment, David looked as if he hadn't understood a single word. Then he made a sound that—understandably—had to be a sigh of relief and nodded.

"I can do that."

"Good," Tommy said. "You keep an eye on the hallway, and if you see or hear even the slightest ..."

"Then I'll come running in here right away to warn you," David concluded for him—and when he saw that Tommy was about to say something more, he added, "And I'll make sure to close the door behind me. Quietly."

Tommy gave his approval with a thumbs up and then turned back towards Randall.

"We'll take one row at a time, you on the right and me on the left, and then move downwards ... how does that sound?"

Randall glanced across the auditorium and was momentarily caught by the large screen on the back wall, where the film's meaningless images still flickered past at such a high speed that it was difficult to distinguish one from the other.

Rorschach tests. That was what it looked like. An endless stream of abstract inkblots like those the psychologists used to find psychological deviations in patients.

An icy cold crept up his spine when he realized that the purpose might be the same here. That someone perhaps was in the process of identifying deviants among the children, using the film as a tool.

It was a frightening thought. Not least because he himself had experienced up close what awaited in this new world for those branded as deviants.

It dawned on him that he hadn't yet answered Tommy's question, but when he turned around to do so, he saw that Tommy had already taken his silence as consent. At least, he had moved to the left side of the room, where he was edging himself forward in the narrow space between the chairs in one of the rows.

Aware that he would have to do so while he could still find the courage, Randall turned around and followed his brother's example on his own side of the auditorium.

Stepping in through the door and spotting the kids in the first place had been bad. But moving through the narrow passage—knowing that he had to look closely at each and every one of those pale, expressionless faces as they slid past—was far worse. Not least because he at the same time hoped and dreaded that one of them would be Billy's.

When he reached the end of the first row, he circled around the outer seat and continued directly onto the next row. Following that pattern, he continued through the rows, and with the exception of a few times, where he jolted because he accidently stroked one of the drop bags with his elbow, he managed to curb his fear surprisingly well.

At least until the moment when his big brother's voice, contorted in a strange mixture between a shout and a whisper, called him over to the other side of the room.

— 26 —

The unnatural pallor of his skin, the purple glow of his lips, and the empty, glass-like eyes made him fall in with all the other children and look like another figure in this horrifying, living wax gallery.

But the freckled boy with the blonde hair and the striped T-shirt *was* Billy. They had found him. Some version of him, at least.

"What have they done to you?" Randall tried to say, but his despair suffocated the words and made them sound as if he was trying to speak through a pillow.

Not that it would have made any difference. Billy reacted neither to Randall's voice nor the touch as he laid his quivering hand on his cheek. He just stared blankly up at the blobs of ink that were still whipping by up on the canvas. Just like the girl had done over on the other side. And just like all the other kids were still doing.

"Are you sure that's a good idea?" Tommy asked,

as Randall grabbed the shutting mechanism at the end of the plastic hose, intending to pull the drop's needle out of the boy's arm. "What if they ... need it?"

Randall hesitated, but only for a moment, because even though the drop bag on the pole behind Billy's seat was almost completely empty, a few of the small, dark gray shadows were still swimming around in the liquid inside. And he had no intention of leaving the tunnel that gave them free passage down to his son's blood vessels open.

From the hole left by the needle, small, burgundy drops now trickled forth. When there were enough of them, they joined together in two groups and ran down both sides of the boy's thin wrists, forming a macabre bracelet.

But still there was no reaction. Not a whimper, not a twitch. Nothing.

"Hey, BumbleBilly," Randall whispered as he slid his arms under the boy's armpits and locked his hands in a braided grip behind his back. "It's okay, honey. Dad is here. We are ... we are going home now."

He tried to lift the boy up and carry him in his arms, as he had done so many times before, but Billy's limp body made it an almost impossible task. It was like carrying around a life-size water balloon that slipped out in all the places where there wasn't direct support.

The fact that his own body still hurt from the injuries it had suffered during the showdown on Highway 55 didn't help either, and after the third unsuccessful attempt, Randall had to give up and put the boy back in the seat.

For a moment, this defeat was dangerously close to pushing him over the edge to a new breakdown, but then Tommy came to his rescue once again.

"You'll never get him all the way out to the car like that," he said. "But if you give us a moment, David and I can get the wheelchair we saw in the storage room."

Not being able to carry his own son out was an immensely bitter pill to swallow, but there was simply no time to dwell on it, so Randall forced it down and nodded.

"Just hurry."

"We will."

With those words, Tommy turned around and edged out to the center aisle between the rows of chairs. When he got out there, he picked up speed and ran up to David, who was still guarding the doorway. The two of them exchanged a few words that Randall was too far away to hear, after which they snuck the door open and disappeared into the corridor.

While he waited for their return, Randall made a few more attempts to get through to Billy, but none of the words he uttered spawned any kind of reaction, and he ended up sitting in silence with Billy's hand in his.

It felt cold, and he wondered—though he told himself not to—whether it would ever get warm again.

And if it would ever again catch a baseball.

An eternity later, the doors opened once more, and Tommy came in. He brought the wheelchair and pushed it in front of him while David stood behind and made sure it went free of the doors.

When they had gotten all the way in, Tommy

continued down to Randall while David resumed his job as a watchkeeper.

"It creaks and it's a little shaky," Tommy said, parking the wheelchair at the end of the row Randall and Billy were in. "But it should do the trick."

"It's brilliant," groaned Randall, who had already picked up Billy and was in the process of carrying him to the chair. "Besides, we can't afford to be picky, now can we, Billy?"

"I don't think he can ..." Tommy began, but then he went silent and instead spent his energy helping to get the boy in place.

The wheelchair seat had a fixed harness that was really meant to sit across the patient's belly, but because Billy was so small and thin, they could give him a little extra support by sliding the harness up over the chair's handle on one side so it could tighten across his chest, just as the seat belt in a car would do.

"DROP IT!"

In a moment of confusion, Randall thought Tommy's outburst was directed at him, and he stared down at his hands, which had just released the buckle of the harness and therefore were empty. Then he shook his head and instead let his gaze slide upwards.

The first thing he saw was the rifle, which no longer hung on Tommy's shoulder, but was instead held in a tight grip by his hands. The next thing was the person the barrel of the rifle was aimed at.

As he stood there in the doorway at one of the auditorium's other entrances, the paramedic was hard to miss. Firstly, the flickering light from the movie screen was constantly captured and thrown back by his bright yellow reflective vest, and secondly, half of his face was clearly lit up by the mobile phone he held up to his ear.

"I SAID DROP IT!" Tommy repeated as he walked over to the man. "WHAT ARE YOU, DEAF? LET GO OF THE FUCKING PHONE!"

The man looked around as if to assess whether it would be possible to escape. Apparently, he came to the conclusion that it wouldn't, because now he held one hand up in front of himself and the other—the one with the phone—out to the side as if to signal that he was going to put it down.

By pointing the rifle's barrel down at the floor in front of the man's feet, Tommy motioned for him to put it there.

The man followed the order and slowly bent down. But then, just as he had placed the phone on the floor, he did something completely unexpected. He kicked it, making it slide across the floor with a scraping sound and then disappear into the shadows under the chairs.

"Oh, you *really* shouldn't have done that," Tommy hissed, and for a moment the anger in his voice made Randall think he might actually pull the trigger. Especially if the fool in the reflective vest should decide to try his luck and run away.

None of it happened. Tommy kept his finger in check, and the paramedic remained still with his hands up in the air until they had come all the way over to him.

"Why did you do that?" Tommy asked. "Who were you talking to?"

The man remained silent, but pulled his lips up in a defiant smile, reminiscent of that which one of the police officers at the gas station had given them, while saying they would never get away with their plans.

Yet, there was the significant difference that the officer's smile at the time had seemed somewhat more convincing. Maybe because he had a service gun, while the only thing hanging from this chubby paramedic's belt was a large bundle of keys.

"You might as well tell us. We'll find out in a minute anyway."

That was David who had joined them without Randall noticing. He was walking along the end wall, looking under the seats in the area where the phone ended up.

"Who were you calling?" Tommy tried again, but when silence—and the condescending smile—was still the only answer, he quickly turned his attention to Randall.

"What should we do with him?"

Randall shrugged and then motioned for Tommy to come closer so they could talk undisturbed.

When Tommy had walked over to him, they both turned around. Not so far that they had their backs to the man and thus couldn't keep an eye on him, but far enough to create some kind of privacy.

"What do you suggest?" Tommy whispered.

"To be completely honest, I really don't care what we do to him. All I care about is getting Billy out of here."

That wasn't completely true. Sure, he was eager to get out, but he hadn't quite reached the point where all moral considerations could be pushed aside. For though the man with the reflective vest had obviously played a part in what was going on in here, Randall was also aware it probably wasn't something the man did of his own free will. That there was something or someone who brain-washed him, just as there had been something or someone who made the blank into what they were now.

"We can't risk letting him go," Tommy concluded. "That's for sure. And knocking him out is not a very good solution either, because if he wakes up again and sounds the alarm before we're out, we're in trouble. It's also too risky to start tying him up in here, because we have to assume that the doctors will return soon to check on the kids, and if they spot us, we're ... yeah, in even more trouble."

"The storage room? There were lots of things on the shelves that we could use to tie him up."

"That might not be such a bad idea."

"Whatever you decide, it's got to be fast," David said behind them. "We're running out of time."

"What do you mean?"

"'Check the last call," David said, reaching out his hand. In it lay the paramedic's mobile phone with the call log open on the screen.

Randall and Tommy read the top item on the list, and both formed the same swear word with their lips.

911—EMERGENCY LINE.

— 27 —

David was right. The paramedic's emergency call meant that time had become a very critical factor.

The first police sirens could be heard in the distance, even before Tommy pulled the box of bandage rolls down from the shelf and ripped it open. And now that he had used most of the bandages to tie the paramedic to the shelves in the small storage room, several new police cars had joined the wailing siren chorus.

Amazingly, Tommy had managed to remain calm despite these distant howls from the pack of big city wolves, who undoubtedly were heading in their direction. His hands shook, yes, but he took the time to tighten and double-check all the knots thoroughly before he got up and nodded.

"Now he's not going anywhere. Isn't that right, Captain?"

Above the tight bandages covering his mouth, the paramedic's eyes were reduced to two narrow cracks, and he tried—without success—to break free from the makeshift straitjacket.

"An impressive piece of work," Randall said, patting his brother on the shoulder. "Now, let's get the heck away from here."

"Shouldn't we mark the door or something?" asked David, who was standing next to Billy's wheelchair a few feet behind the others. "Just so we're sure he's found and doesn't ... you know, rot in here."

"Good idea," Randall said, looking around the room until his gaze caught a mop leaning against the wall in one of the corners. "Maybe you can use that?"

David accepted the proposal and immediately set about making a display that would be hard to miss. He collected a bunch of cardboard boxes from the shelves, stacked them in the middle of the corridor, and then clamped the floor mop in between the door and its frame so it was held ajar.

After taking one last look at David's work—and at their prisoner behind the small window in the door—the group began to walk back towards the hospital entrance. They chose a different route than the one they had followed earlier; partly because they could access the green area directly from the ground floor of this building and thus get back to the entrance hall faster—and partly because David wasn't excited about having to cross the bridge again.

How much time they had spent in the aisles and rooms of Newcrest Memorial Hospital only really dawned on Randall when they stepped out of the glass door and into the green area. The sky was still cloudy, but it was no longer a light, pearly gray color that the clouds were painted with. It was a sad and dark gray twilight color.

The rain had also returned. Not big, heavy drops like the icicles that had whipped down on him on Highway 55, but big enough to leave them well and thoroughly soaked if they took too much time traversing the paths in the green area.

With that in mind, Randall tightened his grip on the wheelchair handles and leaned down towards Billy.

"Hold on tight, honey," he said, ignoring the

compassionate look it triggered from David. "I'm gonna have to speed up a bit so we don't get too wet, okay?"

While they ran, as fast as the wet grass allowed, across the green area, the sound of the sirens continued to increase in strength, and upon entering the entrance hall, they were met by red and blue lights, flashing somewhere out on the other side of the large windows.

"Why the hell didn't we park closer?" Tommy groaned as he stopped in front of the glass doors leading out to the parking lot.

So far, there was only one patrol car out there, but if the sound was any indication, it had backup on the way that would be arriving in the very near future. Large-scale backup.

"Can we sneak out there without being seen?" David asked, and Tommy immediately shook his head.

"It's too risky. The car is too far away."

"If we run?"

Tommy raised one eyebrow and nodded towards the wheelchair as if to say: *Run? Hauling that?*

"Our best chance is for you to wait here while I slip out and get the car."

Randall felt the urge to protest, and under different circumstances he probably would have. Right now, however, he was standing with his hands on the handles of the wheelchair in which his son was sitting—and he had no intention of letting go of those handles for a single second until Billy was safe. Besides, it was difficult to challenge Tommy's point. After all, three men and a kid in a wheelchair would be much easier to spot in the empty parking lot than a single person.

"You stay on standby in here," Tommy said, underlining by the tone of his voice that the debate was over, and the decision had been made. "I'll drive as close to the entrance as I can and as soon as I stop ..."

"Then we jump in the car," Randall concluded. "We know. Now get out of here before more guests arrive."

Hardly had he said those words before one more pair of flashing blue lights joined those belonging to the first responder out in the parking lot. On the plus side, both patrol cars were a good distance away from Tommy's Chevrolet. Nonetheless, it was worrying that there were now two he needed to sneak past.

At least the rain will make him harder to spot, Randall thought, as he and David from their place behind the windows in the entrance hall watched Tommy sneak out and begin to move across the large open space.

And the rain was, Randall quickly ascertained, an advantage for Tommy. One thing was that it put a foggy veil over everything, but the large amount of water on their windshields also had to make it harder for the officers in the patrol cars to see what was going on outside.

When Tommy—now nothing more than a foggy silhouette—had gotten about halfway over to the car, Randall felt a cold fear creeping up his spine. This time it wasn't one, but three new patrol cars joining the party. And he could have sworn that one of them had caught Tommy in the cones of the headlights as it turned into the parking lot.

"He really didn't see him?" asked David, who had apparently made the same observation.

Randall shrugged and was about to say he had thought the same thing when a new—and even more worrying—question struck him.

"Why aren't they coming out?"

"What do you mean?"

"They just stay in their cars. Why aren't they stepping out?"

Below his tousled hair, David's eyes were momentarily confused. Then something dawned in them, and he made a nervous, hissing sound.

"Because they know he's going to come to them? Because it's a trap?"

"Because it's a trap," Randall repeated, nodding.

Or they could just be waiting for the rest of the team to show up. Have you thought about that?

Allie's suggestion sounded reasonable but felt wrong. Because why would they need more than the five patrol cars that were out there now when they could see that Tommy's Chevrolet was the only civilian vehicle in the parking lot?

He turned around to share this thought with

David, but was instantly interrupted by a sound that cut through the noise from the sirens and made the hairs on the back of his neck rise.

It came from the parking lot, and even though the sound was only there for a fleeting second before it disappeared again, he had no doubt as to what created it.

He looked out the window and immediately had his terrible premonition confirmed.

A large police dog—a German Shepherd judging by its size and posture—had been let loose out in the parking lot. It was now moving in Tommy's direction at such a breakneck speed that it looked like it was hovering above the asphalt.

Run, Tommy, run goddammit! Randall screamed in his thoughts, as if he had an irrational expectation that the words could reach Tommy via some telepathic connection they had never explored, if he just made sure to shout them loud enough inside his head.

Tommy hardly needed the extra encouragement, though. He had spotted the four-legged beast and was now running, as fast as he could, towards the car.

He had a head start and clearly gave everything he had in him, not to waste it. The only problem was that the dog was unnervingly agile, and when there were only a few yards left between him and the car door, it caught up with him—and then it jumped.

It hit him at chest height with such force that he toppled over on the asphalt. Then it grabbed his leg and began to pull at him, as if it was trying to drag him all the way back to the officers in the patrol cars.

It was his imagination, it had to be, but for a moment Randall's brain insisted that he could hear both its growl and the sound of Tommy's clothes being ripped to pieces as he was pulled across the asphalt.

What, on the other hand, wasn't his imagination was the shrill whine that the dog now exhaled as Tommy lifted his free leg and kicked it on the nose.

The pain caused the beast to let go of his leg and stagger a few feet back, but Tommy's freedom was short-lived, for it didn't take many seconds for the

German Shepherd to find its balance again. And when it did, it changed—probably to disorient its prey—strategy. It began to jump feverishly from side to side while barking and snapping at him.

The strategy worked. An opening was created, which the beast immediately used to clamp itself onto Tommy's arm.

In a desperate attempt to turn the attack to his advantage, Tommy grabbed the dog's body and pulled it with him as he rolled sideways. The result was that both he and the animal fell out of sight because they disappeared in the shadows in front of the car.

And it was then—in the long seconds that followed, where there was no movement to be seen—that the balance finally tipped in the scales of Randall's conscience.

"I can't just stand here and watch. I have to help him."

He expected to be met by protest. That David would point out that he was only a teenager and couldn't carry the responsibility of taking care of Billy alone, or that he would suggest that he himself went out there instead. But David surprised him. He just nodded and put his hands on the wheelchair's handles.

Five steps. That was what Randall managed to take in the direction of the door before the sound of a loud bang coming from the parking lot outside made him stiffen.

A shot. Someone had fired a weapon out there.

With his heart pounding wildly against the ribs in his chest, he turned around and looked out the window.

The first place his gaze sought was the right side of the parking lot, where all the patrol cars had gathered in a semicircle. The tangle of blue and red colors flashing on their roofs made it difficult to focus properly, but apart from the officer who had released the dog, no one else appeared to have left their cars.

Apparently, these psychopaths were just planning to sit in the front seats of their cars, safe from the rain, and enjoy the show while their furry killing machine ripped the deviant to pieces. As if they were spectators in some insane mixture of a gladiator arena and a drive-in cinema.

From the patrol cars, Randall's gaze slid further into the center of the parking lot, where Tommy's Chevrolet was parked. And as his eyes found it, a wave of almost euphoric relief washed through him.

Yes, goddammit! Come on!

Tommy was on his feet again—and he must have managed to open the car door, because there was light inside the cabin. The police dog was still there, and still snapping at him, but not at all with the same eagerness as before. It was clear that it had been intimidated by the loud bang—which Randall now understood came from Tommy's rifle and not one of the officers' service weapons.

The same rifle Tommy now used as a club to keep the animal at bay while he backed into the front seat of the car.

When he had gotten all the way in, he averted one last attack by hammering the shaft of the rifle into the neck of the mutt, after which he quickly pulled back the rifle and slammed the door.

"Did he make it?" David asked.

"I think so."

Randall squinted his eyes, hesitated for a moment, then nodded.

"Yep, he's starting the car now. We gotta get to the door."

"Oh, yeah, of course," David said, after which he pulled the wheelchair back a little, turned it around, and pushed it in front of him as he ran over to the front doors.

Meanwhile, Randall cast one last glance out into the parking lot where Tommy had just turned on the headlights.

The feeling that there was something wrong with what he saw out there hit him almost immediately, but for the first few seconds he couldn't identify the cause.

Then it came to him: Two of the patrol cars had turned off both their headlights and the flashing lights on the roof, leaving them almost completely invisible, engulfed by the rain and the darkness.

And as Tommy stepped on the gas pedal and started driving, the two darkened patrol cars did the same.

— 28 —

In reality, the horrible scenario in its entirety was played out over no more than a few seconds. But from the moment he saw the first patrol car crash into the back of Tommy's Chevrolet, Randall felt as if someone had turned a knob that made time go slower. As if some loathsome higher power had decided to play the scene as a slow-motion sequence in a movie, so there really was time to take it all in.

And there was. Randall caught details he shouldn't have been able to. He saw small sparks shoot up into the air like fireworks as the metal in the patrol car's radiator grille met the metal on the rear left side of Tommy's car and caused it to slide sideways across the asphalt. And when the car's rotation stopped about ten yards from the front of the hospital, he noticed that half of the Chevy's bumper had curled up in an arc above the trunk—and he even had time to think that it looked like a scorpion's tail.

When the other darkened patrol car appeared seconds later—and hit cleanly in the middle of the same side—Randall saw his brother press one hand against the ceiling and the other against the dashboard in a desperate attempt to stay in place while the car tipped over onto its roof. He also saw him open his mouth in a scream that couldn't be heard because it was drowned out by the creaking sound from the car's body as it was pushed across the asphalt.

All of these awful details Randall observed through the strange, dreamy slow-motion filter, but at the moment when Tommy's car—sideways and still turned upside down—slammed through the glass doors in the hospital entrance, time suddenly went back to normal.

"Get Billy out of here!" he shouted to David while he himself ran to the car and slid down on his knees in front of the side window. The pane was still there, but the glass was cracked in so many places that it looked like a spider's web. Behind the glass, Tommy hung in the seat belt with his head downwards. There were bloody wounds on his hands and a deep cut in his forehead over one of the eyebrows, but he was—and this was the most important thing—conscious.

Confused and injured, yes ... but also alive and conscious.

After two unsuccessful attempts at opening the door, Randall concluded that it had bent too much during the slide so it simply couldn't be done. He would have to get Tommy out through the window.

He knocked on the glass and signaled him to protect his face.

Tommy nodded and twisted his upper body around in the seat, so he had his back to the windowpane—and then Randall kicked.

The first kick gave the pane's cobweb pattern a few extra threads, and the next caused all the threads to break at the same time, thereby bursting the glass.

"Can you reach the buckle?" Randall asked as he struck pieces of glass still hanging in the window's rubber frames off with his elbow.

Tommy raised his arm, grimaced, raised it a little more and grimaced again. He kept on like that until his hand reached the buckle's release button.

Although Randall tried to support him to soften the fall, Tommy clearly got hurt when his shoulder and back landed on top of the many glass splinters. He didn't scream, but his lips trembled, and his breathing got fast and uneven.

"Can you turn around so you can crawl out?"

"Just ... give me ... a moment."

"I can't, Tommy. We don't have time. The dog and the officers are still out there, and they are on their way in here."

Apparently the thought of the furry beast was the spark needed to wake up Tommy, who with an awkward movement kicked his legs sideways so they came to lie on the inside of the car's roof over the passenger seat. Then he turned around and be-gan—with Randall's help—to crawl out through the broken side window.

"You are doing fine. Just a little bit more. Come on, you can do it."

Randall did what he could, but it wasn't super easy to give an optimistic pep-talk when a thick, dark gray smoke had begun to ooze out of the vent grate, while the sound of distant voices outside revealed that the policemen had gotten out of the cars. Company was on its way.

As an unnerving confirmation of that thought, he heard a series of clicking sounds right on the other side of the car.

Paws on asphalt. *Claws* on asphalt.

He listened, tried to pinpoint where the dog was at, but the sound had already died out.

For a few seconds there was complete silence, and then the claws suddenly returned. This time it just wasn't the asphalt they were scraping against, but rather the cracked window by the passenger seat behind Tommy. The beast was literally trying to dig its way in via the window.

At first, Randall didn't understand why it didn't just run around or jump over the car, but as he leaned to the side, he saw it immediately: Tommy's Chevrolet had smashed the entrance doors, but it hadn't broken all the way through, and now it was caught, tightly, between the two walls.

However, the protection the car wreck gave them wouldn't last very long. On the one hand, the glass of the pane creaked uneasily under the paws of the police dog, and on the other hand, the gray smoke from the vent was starting to get an uncanny orange glow. If that meant what Randall feared—that something had caught fire in the engine—the shit was about to hit the fan very soon.

Using that thought as a driving force, he held out his hand to Tommy, who grabbed it and then let himself be pulled the rest of the way out the window in one quick jerk.

Behind Tommy, the dog snarled and scratched even harder on the window when it saw its prey being pulled away, but even though it creaked and squeaked, the glass didn't yield.

Tommy staggered a bit and had to lean on Randall's shoulder, but once he'd gotten up, he was able to put one foot in front of the other and keep a reasonable speed as they moved over towards the doors leading into the central corridor. The same door Randall had seen David and Billy run through a while ago.

The door was ajar, and David must have been watching them through the narrow opening, because as soon as they reached it, he pushed the door open and almost pulled them into the corridor.

Barely had the door been shut behind them before there was another bang and another clatter of glass coming from the hospital's entrance hall.

The closed door prevented Randall from looking out there, but it wasn't hard to imagine what had happened. One of the officers must have sent a bullet through one of the large windows next to the car wreck, thus opening a new way into the entrance hall for both two- and four-legged members of the police force.

A few seconds later, this theory was confirmed when the same clicking sound as he had heard earlier resounded in the entrance hall—this time accompanied by a deep, throaty growl, which rose alarmingly quickly in volume.

Instinctively, Randall's gaze slid down to the two metal plates sitting under the door handles on either side of the double door. As expected, neither of them had anything reminiscent of a locking mechanism.

"Help me with this," he said, pressing his shoulder against the left side of the double door and motioning for David to do the same on the right side.

It was a solution about as durable as pissing your pants to keep warm in a blizzard, and he knew it. Because even though they were probably able to keep the dog out, it wouldn't be long before the officers also entered the entrance hall. And then the situation would be completely different. But that was ...

Now the blow came—and there was far more power behind it than he had imagined. The beast practically hurled its body into the doors, and for a second an opening was created. Not big enough for it to squeeze through, but enough to give them a glimpse of its spit-glistening, yellow set of teeth.

"For fuck's sake," David almost sobbed. "If we don't find something to keep it closed, we're done for."

"Working on it," Tommy's voice sounded behind them, and as Randall looked back over his shoulder, he could see that Tommy was in the process of pulling his belt free of his jeans.

As soon as it was off, Tommy ran to the door and

used the belt to tie the two door handles together, while Randall and David put all their strength into keeping the doors still.

"There. You can let go now."

Randall and David exchanged a worried look, nodded to each other, and then gradually released the handles.

It seemed to hold. Yes, it shook in the hinges, and there was a small opening between the two doors wide enough to give them another glimpse of the police dog's eerie teeth—as well as a glimpse of a human figure stepping in through the window that had been opened with a bullet ... but it seemed to hold.

"What now?" David asked as the three of them backed away from the door and then started running down the corridor. "What the hell are we going to do?"

Rather than answering the question, Randall tightened his grip on the handles of Billy's wheelchair and put extra force into pushing it. He did it partly because his primary focus right now was to put distance between them and the door, and partly because he had no idea what to answer. With Billy in the wheelchair, escaping on foot was simply not an option—and their getaway car lay in the entrance hall with its wheels pointing upwards like a helpless turtle, overturned on its shell.

"Without a car, we're screwed," Tommy groaned as an echo of Randall's thoughts. "Fucking hell!"

"What about the other side of the hospital?" David suggested. "If we're lucky, there might be another parking lot back there."

Randall shook his head and was about to say they probably wouldn't find any cars since the hospital wasn't even staffed anymore. Then it struck him: it *was* staffed. They had seen several workers over in the other building. One of them they had even tied up and left in the small storage room. A man who had a large bundle of keys hanging in his belt and was wearing a yellow reflective vest with the title: *PARAMEDIC*.

So, assuming that this man had arrived in an ambulance didn't seem unreasonable.

"Why are you slowing down?"

Randall heard the question but didn't answer

Tommy until he had finished skimming for potential exits on the right side of the corridor.

"I'm looking for a way out to the green area, so we can get back to the other building again from there. We need to go back to the storage room."

Tommy stared at him for a moment, obviously perplexed. Then the penny dropped.

"The paramedic?"

Randall nodded, and so did Tommy.

"Few and far between," he said. "But you do have your moments, dear brother. Let's go."

— 29 —

The chubby man in the yellow reflective vest didn't seem to have fought very hard to get rid of the makeshift straitjacket Tommy had made for him with the bandages.

In fact, he mostly looked as if he had given up. He sat with his head bent forward and his shoulders hanging limply. And though a small movement of the head told them he had registered their return, it didn't trigger any noticeable interest in his drowsy eyes.

He didn't react either, when Randall gently reached out and loosened the carabiner locking the large bundle of keys to his belt.

Among the many keys in the bundle, one caught his eye; a large, bulky car key that bore Henry Ford's famous signature, written in white on an oval, dark-blue background.

Randall showed it to David and Tommy, who both nodded. Then he turned his hand and held the key in front of the paramedic's face.

"I'm guessing this fits in an ambulance. Is that correct?"

No response. Not surprising, but also not very worrying. If there actually was an ambulance parked somewhere outside, there was a fair chance that this was the right key, and then the remote would help them find it with or without his help.

Assuming it would just lead to the same result, Randall didn't bother to ask the man where the ambulance was parked. Instead, he put the keys in his pocket, got up, and gestured for the others to follow him.

Outside, in the wide corridor running between the storage room and the auditorium, they stood still for a moment, trying to figure out the best route to take. They had to take the time to do so, even though the sound of voices and occasional barks told them that their pursuers were right on their heels. If the dog and the officers weren't already in the same building as them, they were at least very close.

"I think we need to go back to the building on the

other side," Randall said, pointing down a narrow aisle he believed would take them in that direction. "That was where we spotted the paramedic in the first place, and I think I saw a sign for the Emergency Room over there. It would make sense that he would have parked the ambulance there, right?"

"It totally makes sense," said Tommy, who had volunteered to push Billy's wheelchair for a while so he could lean on it as they walked.

"So ... back across the bridge?"

Randall answered David's question with a shrug and a guilty expression.

"Sorry, kid," Tommy added. "But like it or not, I think you'll just have to bite that apple."

David closed his eyes and kept them closed for a couple of seconds while he took a deep breath. Then he shook it off, put on a determined expression, and started walking.

The same determination was glowing in his eyes when they reached the double door leading to the bridge—and contrary to what Randall had expected, the young man didn't hesitate to push the door open and step out on the walkway.

Admittedly, his hands trembled a little, and under the edge of his hood, which had been pulled up again, some of his hair clung to a sweaty forehead. But he didn't hesitate. Not even with the wind and rain now whipping violently against the windows, making the walkway seem even narrower than before.

Seeing the young man suppress his fear of heights and force himself to move forward made a big impression on Randall. Not least because David's courage seemed to spread to both Tommy and himself. So much so that Randall actually started to believe they might escape the hospital with their lives.

But then came the darkness.

At first, when noticing that the fluorescent tube above them flashed a single time and began to buzz, he read nothing into it. Only when several of the other lamps in the ceiling also started flashing irregularly, and he heard loud clicking noises echoing through the corridors, did it dawn on him what was happening.

Someone was flicking off the lights in the

hospital's main relay.

He looked out through the walkway's windows and had his suspicion confirmed. Section after section on floor after floor was going dark in the building they had just left.

And it was heading their way.

"No, no, no! This just isn't happening!"

The hollow sound of David's voice almost caused physical pain in Randall's heart, and when he turned around and saw that the boy's determined look had been substituted with one of pure horror, it was almost more than he could take.

"Hey, David," he whispered, snapping his fingers. "Look at me. Take a deep breath and don't ..."

No further did he get in his reassuring speech before another click resounded through the air and the walkway fell into darkness. The only remaining light now was what little the garden lights from the green area below them emitted.

No, that wasn't the entire truth. There were two more light sources, but neither of them was especially reassuring. One was the occasional flash of light that appeared in the windows of the hospital when officers passed by with their flashlights. The other was some scattered strokes of lightning, born from the storm in the distance, that for a few milliseconds at a time colored the sky above them a bluish white.

"Get moving, Randall. We have to get out of here!"

Tommy's outburst hit—and awakened—Randall, as if it were a slap in the face. He reached out and grabbed the shoulder of David—who right now was nothing more than a blurred outline of a human figure—and pulled him along.

Stumbling, fumbling, and way too slowly, they moved to the end of the walkway, while the sound of the officers' voices and the dog's barking continued to increase in volume somewhere behind them.

When they reached the end of the walkway, Tommy spun the wheelchair around and backed the remaining distance so he could use his back to push the doors. That way he could pry them open and make sure the coast was clear before entering.

The aisle they stepped into had also gone dark

just a few seconds after the walkway, but at least there was a bit of light to navigate by; more precisely, a large, luminous sign with the words *EMERGENCY EXIT*.

Obviously, the sign was being powered by a separate power source, and even though the faint, green glow it emitted didn't exactly bathe the hallway in light, it still felt as if someone up above had sent them a minor miracle.

Because one thing was certain: If they were planning to find the Emergency Room, they would first and foremost need to get downstairs—and where there was an EMERGENCY EXIT, chances were that there would also be a staircase.

As fast as the darkness allowed, they moved in the direction of the sign, making an effort to steer clear of trolleys, coffee tables, and the like.

Given the circumstances, it went okay. On one occasion, the footplate of the wheelchair bumped against the edge of a bed someone had left carelessly in the middle of the hallway. It made a bit of a noise and had them all gasping, but luckily it didn't seem as if the sound was loud enough to reveal their position to their pursuers.

"It would have been a hell of a lot easier with an elevator," Tommy sighed, as he stopped in front of the emergency exit sign and opened the door, which indeed led into a staircase. A staircase they had to use to cross four floors—in the dark and towing a wheelchair. So yes, an elevator would have been preferable.

"You still got your phone on you?"

Tommy nodded and Randall turned to face David.

"Can you help me get the wheelchair down the stairs if Tommy lights our way?"

David nodded and then walked a few steps down the stairs so he could get a grip at the front of the wheelchair.

"Here?"

"A bit further up, I think. There's a crossbar under the seat."

"This one?"

"Yup. Tommy, what's the status on the light?"

Tommy answered, not using words, but by turning on the phone and directing it at his own face so it was lit up by the glare from the screen. Then he nodded and turned the light down towards the steps.

"If you open the camera app and turn on the flash, you can get more light," David whispered.

"Yeah, I know," Tommy replied. "But it's too risky. They'll see us coming a mile away."

"Fair point."

Although they worked together to keep it balanced, getting the wheelchair down the stairs was no easy task. Especially since the sparse light from the phone's screen was only enough to illuminate a small radius around Tommy, which meant he practically had to move the light every time one of them took a step.

Despite these challenges, they slowly but surely moved down to the landing on the third floor, where they took a short break before continuing.

When they had gotten about halfway down to the landing on the second floor, Randall once again signaled for them to stop. This time, however, it wasn't to get a break. It was because he had picked up something at the edge of his field of vision, a movement of some kind, a little further down the stairs. Maybe it was just something he imagined, but as long as …

Now it came back, and this time he saw it clearly: A square spot of light that faded in on the wall on one side and grew larger, before then disappearing again.

The light from a flashlight shining through the small window in the door to the second floor.

Randall held his breath and focused on listening, trying to separate the sounds.

Footsteps. Two, maybe three people. No growling or barking—and no claws clicking against the floor.

A second group? Maybe.

While they stood there, frozen halfway down a dark and steep staircase, balancing a wheelchair that got heavier with each passing second, another square-shaped spot of light grew on the wall. This one stayed longer than the first one. Long enough for Randall to feel confident that the door would soon be ripped open. But then the light was suddenly gone again—and when it had disappeared, it didn't take long before the sounds also died out.

He waited, listened, waited a little longer, and then let out a long sigh.

"That was damn close," Tommy whispered as he turned on his cell phone and lit the steps in front of the wheelchair.

"Too close," David replied. "And it feels like my forearms are burning."

"Yeah, mine too," Randall said. "The wheelchair isn't exactly easy to balance around. But we can take a break down on the next landing."

David considered for a moment, then shook his head.

"I think we should just keep going and continue all the way down so we can find that ambulance and get away from here."

"Fair enough. Then I just hope I remembered correctly about that sign, and it doesn't turn out that the Emergency Room was actually located in the building we came from."

Even in the darkness, Randall was pretty sure he could see the young man's face turn pale under the hood.

"Seriously?" David moaned. "You're telling me that you're not even ..."

"Don't worry, I'm pretty sure," Randall interrupted.

And he was.

Pretty sure.

— 30 —

Randall wasn't mistaken, and his memory hadn't failed him. It was in this part of the hospital the Emergency Room was located—and shortly after stepping out on the main corridor of the ground floor they were even lucky enough to find a sign telling them where they needed to go in order to find it.

As for their pursuers, the goddess of fortune had also smiled on them so far. To be fair, they had heard the police dog barking once or twice, but it was somewhere far behind, perhaps even all the way up on another floor. They also hadn't heard the officers' voices or seen any light cones from their flashlights sweep across the walls of the corridor.

"Watch out over here," sounded from somewhere in the dark further ahead. "I almost walked straight into it."

It was David's voice. After the stairs, he had taken the lead, while Tommy went back to pushing—and leaning on—the wheelchair.

Along with the temporary leader's role, David had also been given the responsibility to light their way with Tommy's mobile phone—which he now used to show them what it was he had almost walked into: A large, bulky block of a machine, filled with buttons, hoses and shiny metal rods.

Behind the device was an empty hospital bed with the rail folded down. The sheet hung so far down over the edge that it almost reached the floor, and for a brief, but uncomfortable moment, Randall's writer's brain presented him with an entire palette of heinous surprises that could be hiding under that sheet.

"Thank you, David," he whispered back. "We'll make sure to steer clear."

David didn't answer. His full attention was focused on the wide double door he had just opened. And on what he had found behind it.

"Yeah, man," he whispered, while clapping his one hand softly against the top of the doorframe, as if giving it a highfive. "Hell yeah, guys! We found it."

"The ER?"

David responded by giving both doors an extra push at the same time, making them swing open like the doors of a western saloon. Then he made an exaggerated, sweeping motion with his hand, as if he were a butler, inviting them into a large mansion.

The room behind the door wasn't the hall of a large mansion, and there were no Persian rugs on the floors, expensive portraits or hunting trophies on the walls.

But as far as the view was concerned, the Emergency Room's reception at Newcrest Memorial Hospital had no problem competing with any given mansion in Randall's eyes. For behind the furniture in the room—four rows of plastic chairs bolted to the floor—were two sliding glass doors leading out of the building. And behind those, beneath the light cone of a streetlamp, it was parked.

The ambulance. A Ford, mind you.

With shaking fingers, he pulled the car key out of his pocket and pressed the remote.

Two loud beeps—a little louder than he cared

for—cut through the sound of the gushing wind on the other side of the sliding doors. Then the lights flashed a few times at the back of the ambulance, while the side mirrors automatically unfolded.

Randall cast an evaluating glance at his brother. He tried to do it discreetly, but Tommy saw it and answered the question in his mind with an offended snort.

"If I was able to walk all the way over here, I'm probably able to step on a fucking pedal, don't you think?" he scoffed, holding out his hand.

Randall sent him a grateful smile and then let the keys fall into Tommy's palm. Next, he went over and pulled one of the sliding doors aside. With no power, he had to do it manually, but luckily it still glided smoothly in its rails, so he managed to do it without too much noise.

Outside, the rain had calmed a bit, but the wind was still bitterly cold as it poured in through the opening and surrounded him.

After creating a gap large enough for the wheelchair to get through, he proceeded to the ambulance and opened its back doors.

"Is there enough room for us to bring the wheel-chair?" Tommy whispered.

"I think so," Randall replied, pulling himself up into the ambulance so he could a better look. "There will be, for sure, if we remove the stretcher and the ... oxygen thingy."

"Then get it done. In the meantime, I'll check to see if this thing's still alive."

With those words, Tommy walked over to the side of the vehicle, entered, and sat down in the driver's seat. In the meantime, Randall turned to David to ask if he could help him carry the stretcher out.

Only he didn't even manage to open his mouth before he had forgotten all about what he was go-ing to say.

The police dog was back. It had caught up with them and was now standing right in the middle of the doorway into the Emergency Room.

It looked like something out of a nightmare. The ruffled fur on its back was standing straight up, its teeth were bared, and despite the distance, Randall was sure he could see all the details in its small, vicious eyes. That he could feel its gaze rest on him.

This last detail was the one thing that didn't bother him now, however. He would at any time prefer that it was his throat—and not Billy's—the beast dreamed of sinking its teeth into.

Not that it makes that much of a difference, he thought, feeling the cold panic pierce his heart like an icicle. *If it starts barking now, none of us will get out of here alive.*

As if it had somehow been able to read this thought in his head, the dog laid its ears all the way down to its head. Next, it bent its knees in the same way Randall had seen wolves do in nature programs when they got ready to howl.

But then, as it turned its head slightly to the right, it suddenly stiffened—and what was probably meant to have been a deafening howl or a threatening snarl came out as a pathetic whimper while its tail slowly found its way in between its back legs.

"What's wrong with it?" Tommy whispered from the front seat of the ambulance as the dog began to stumble backwards through the Emergency Room, and then disappeared out into the hallway from where it had entered.

Randall had no idea. At least that was what he let Tommy believe when he responded with a shrug.

In reality, however, the dog's eyes had revealed part of the explanation to him. Because the mutt had seen something that made it terrified.

And it was Billy that its eyes were fixed on when it happened. Billy, who sat huddled and helpless in the wheelchair with strands of spit dangling down from his chin.

"Well, who even cares why?" Tommy said. "Let's just get the hell out of here before it changes its mind and comes back."

Randall nodded and waved at David to come up and help him remove the stretcher and oxygen machine from the ambulance. When done with that, they lifted the wheelchair up, placed it in the middle of the ambulance floor, and locked both of its wheels. Then they sat down on the plastic seats that were mounted at one side of the vehicle.

Now they sat there, Randall with one hand on

the wheelchair's handle and the other on Billy's arm, David with both hands hanging loosely down between his knees while Tommy put the ambulance in gear and started driving.

For a long time, they stayed just like that—sitting in tense silence with shaking nerves—while they listened intensely for the sound of sirens.

None came.

ACT 4
THE FARM

"I would rip, tear, throw, shot, cut and kill.
Without hesitation, without shame or guilt.
I am a father. What more need you know?"
— O. E. Geralt, Morality, Mortality.

— EPILOGUE —

The old, worn floorboards creak loudly under the weight as Randall pushes Billy's wheelchair over the doorstep and onto the back porch of Tommy's farm.

That—and some birds chirping somewhere out in the cornfield that the porch overlooks—are the only sounds that can be heard this morning.

Billy is also quiet, but that is nothing new. In the five weeks that have passed since they placed him in the wheelchair and drove him out of the auditorium at Newcrest Memorial Hospital, the boy has not uttered a single comprehensible word.

Sounds, yes. Especially at night when he is lying in bed whining softly while Randall alternately strokes the boy's hair and wipes the tears from his own cheeks.

Even when they took him back to his old room in Allie's apartment in Newcrest a few weeks ago, Billy was as silent as the grave. None of the things from his old life that they showed him made an impression. His Playstation 4, his Star Wars action figures, his impressive collection of baseball cards—none of the stuff he would have previously considered his most valuable possessions made an impression. He just stared at it with his empty, expressionless eyes.

Actually, the decision to bring Billy back to the apartment was about something else at first. Because at the time, Randall wasn't aware that Allie had gone, and he hoped that seeing his mother again might ... spark something in the boy.

Oh yeah, well, in truth he also hoped it would work the other way around. That Allie perhaps would break out of her mental prison when she saw that the prodigal son had returned.

But Allie was nowhere to be found—and judging by the state of the apartment, she had been gone for a long time. And there were no signs that she had plans to return. However, that wasn't too surprising, because at that time they had started to notice that a lot of the blank would suddenly disappear when they reached a certain stage in their decay.

Where they went? He had no idea.

"Are you ready for some breakfast?"

It's a rhetorical question, and Randall doesn't wait for an answer before reaching out and grabbing the small bowl of oatmeal standing on the table next to the bench he is sitting on.

He put the bowl out there a while before he went in to get Billy, so the oatmeal has cooled off. Still, he blows on the contents of the spoon before leading it up to the boy's half-open mouth.

When the first spoonful has been carefully poured into his mouth, Billy's tongue appears in the corner of it. There it hangs for a while, after which it slowly retracts. Then he starts chewing. Thank God, he's still able to do that.

"What do you want to do today?" Randall asks. "Of course, we need to look at the thing with the well, like we promised Tommy. But after that, I thought we could watch a movie. Maybe one of the old Star Wars, if you ... if you'd like?"

Billy chews on. Randall bites his lip and nods thoughtfully.

"Then it's a deal, buddy. We fix the filter in the well, and then we'll watch a movie together."

Three mouthfuls of oatmeal later, there has still been no response, but that's okay. Randall is, in his own quiet way, starting to accept that he in many ways is playing ball against a wall.

It's a thought that regularly gnaws like a parasite in the back of his head—and one that can sometimes be almost impossible to get rid of. Today, however, it isn't allowed to get a proper grip in there, as something from the outside manages to steal his attention before it happens.

A movement. Something reddish-brown that shoots up the trunk of the old, moss-covered maple tree in Tommy's garden.

"Oh look, I think we have a guest in the garden," Randall says, after which he bends down and reaches his hand in under the bench. When it reappears, it's holding an old glass jar, filled to the brim with hazelnuts. "Do you think it's Chili?"

Chili is a squirrel that lives in the forest area on the east side of the farm, and in the mornings, it often passes through Tommy's garden in its hunt for food. At first, the animal was very shy, but as it realized that Randall meant it no harm—and that he had a jar full of nuts, which he happily handed out from—it became more and more tame. So tame that after the first fourteen days on the farm he could often lure the squirrel all the way up onto the porch just by shaking the jar, making the nuts rattle.

He does the same now: shakes the jar, waits a bit ... and shakes it again.

Up in the maple tree, the reddish-brown shadow shoots down over the trunk at breakneck speed. About halfway down to the ground, it sets off and flies in an arc down towards the grass. For a few seconds, a ruffled, light brown tail can be clearly seen. Then it disappears down between the blades of grass—to then reappear when Chili dashes up the porch steps and stops a few yards from Randall's feet.

"Well, there she is," Randall exclaims and smiles at Billy, while he unscrews the lid of the jar and pulls out a hazelnut. "Indeed, it was Chili, coming to say hi."

He extends his hand and knocks the nut gently against one of the floorboards, as if he is carrying out some sort of shady trade with the squirrel and wants to reassure her that what is rattling around inside the hard shell is of the highest quality.

Chili's small, black eyes lock onto the nut while she turns her head from side to side and rubs her forepaws together in small, quick movements. Then she jumps forward and stops in front of Randall's hand.

The very second Chili grabs hold of the nut, the shrill sound of a car's horn emerges from the other side of the house.

The sound is unexpected and a stark contrast to this morning's silence, therefore making Randall jump in his seat. The squirrel, on the other hand, is completely unaffected. She only has an eye for her hard-shelled prize, which she now begins to drag with her back to her storage ... wherever that may be.

You are a brave little one, Randall thinks, as Chili once again disappears out of sight amidst the green waves of the garden. Experience tells him she will be back for a refill shortly.

"Did you hear that?" he asks, turning to Billy. "Tommy and David are back."

Nothing. Billy doesn't even turn his head at the sound of his voice anymore.

That's one more thing Randall must learn to live with. That he, in Billy's eyes, is probably just a random stranger who pops up every now and then with food.

It dawns on him that it probably is very similar to the way Chili sees him, and that saddens his heart.

Somewhere inside the house, a door is opened, and soon after, the sound of creaking floorboards, footsteps, and voices follows.

"We are out here! On the porch."

"Just a minute," he hears Tommy shout back. "We just need to unload this."

He sounds jolly. That's good. The trip must have been a success.

Half a minute later, that assumption is confirmed as Tommy shows up in the doorway behind them with a crooked smile on his lips.

"So, how did it go?"

"Better than expected. We were able to fill all our own cans, and then we even found a pallet with eight more. So we are well on our way to keeping the generator running all winter."

"Nice. And what about food?"

"Let's just say you'll be pretty tired of cocktail sausages and canned ham before we reach the spring."

I already am, Randall thinks, but he just shrugs and keeps it to himself.

"We met someone."

"Blank or ...?"

Tommy shakes his head.

"Not blank. They were normal, just like us. Well yeah, as normal as can be after witnessing the end of the world. But they seemed peaceful. At least those who were in the group that we met."

Before continuing, Tommy hesitates, and the cheeky smile from before reappears on his lips.

"One of them was a girl. About David's age. A pretty one."

"Aha," Randall says, making big eyes.

"Yup. You'll never get him to admit it, but he was completely buzzing when we left."

"Do we know where they are staying?"

"No, it was too much to ask for on the first date. For us as well. But they gave us a radio frequency that we can contact them on. They said they keep it open for an hour every afternoon."

"Might come in handy," Randall says. "Especially if they are part of a larger group. Then maybe we can trade with them when the resources start to thin out."

"Or join them, if it comes to that."

"Sure, I guess that's also an option," Randall says, shrugging his shoulders before purposely changing the subject. "So, where did you end up sleeping? The car again, or did you find something better?"

"When we left Newcrest yesterday afternoon, we were completely demolished, so instead of driving all the way home in one stretch, we decided to spend some time finding a good place to spend the night. And David spotted a mansion, hell, more like a castle, really, close to Haywood. So yeah, we slept like kings, I can tell you. With a view of the river and everything."

"Newcrest? I thought you were planning to go west. How did you end up in Newcrest?"

"Had to pick up your present, didn't I?"

"My present?"

Tommy throws on a cryptic smile and raises one eyebrow. Then he disappears—excessively slowly and with wide-open eyes, like a vampire in an old movie pulling into the shadows—back into the doorway.

When he reappears, his hands are holding something—and before Randall's eyes have time to decode what it is, Tommy dumps it onto his lap.

Randall looks down ... and feels his throat tighten.

"You are probably gonna have to find a new folder," Tommy says. "The fire didn't reach the trunk, but the heat did, and the plastic in the cover didn't handle that too well. But I flipped through it, and it looks like the papers survived."

Randall swallows the lump in his throat and nods as he runs his fingertips across the front of the folder as if to check that it's actually there. That it's not just something his brain imagines.

"Well," Tommy says, patting him on the shoulder. "I'd better get back to the car, so David doesn't have to do everything by himself."

Randall raises his head again, their eyes meet, and what needs to be said between the two brothers is said with a grateful smile and a short nod. Then Tommy disappears into the house once more.

Once he is gone, Randall exhales a long sigh and leans back on the bench. He sits like that for a long time, silent and reclined, while he listens to the wind playing with the corn plants out in the field.

And to Billy's heavy breathing.

"This wasn't how I imagined it," he says. "The way I saw it, we were sitting on the edge of the bed in your room, but ..."

He takes a pause and uses it to get his emotions under control. And his voice.

"But this is what we've got. So, it is what it is."

With those words, he gently grabs the corner of the folder's front and opens it.

He reads the words on the first page inside his

head and then tilts the folder so Billy can see them too.

THE LONGEST WAY—BY RANDALL MORGAN.

"It's my new book," he explains. "I finished it just before it all went to hell, and I ... I had thought we perhaps could read it together. That I could read it aloud to you."

From the huddled boy in the wheelchair, no answer comes, but behind the edge of the top step on the porch stairs, a familiar cluster of tousled brown fur emerges. It's Chili who—as expected—has returned to pick up her second ration.

Randall smiles at her as she jumps up the last step and turns her small, beady eyes expectantly towards the glass jar.

He finds a nut, knocks it against the floor as usual ... but then decides that Chili ought to work a little harder for it this time. So, he places the nut on the floor between his feet instead of handing it to her.

Chili stares at him, then at the nut, and then back at him. Then she slowly begins to sneak forward.

Meanwhile, Randall turns his attention back to his son and the book manuscript. He flips to the next page, clears his throat, and begins to read aloud from the dedication.

"For my son, Billy. My little bumblebee. May you, as it does, fly high and safe, even when the world around you tells you that you can't."

The small movement the boy makes with his left hand is almost imperceptible. He opens and closes it, and it only lasts a fraction of a second. But that one fraction of a second is enough for Randall to register it out of the corner of his eye. Enough to make him stiffen and feel his whole world narrow down to one single thought:

It can't be, it must be something you imagined.

But no, as he turns his head and takes a closer look at his son's hand, he realizes it's not just his imagination. Because the movement returns. It comes in small, short waves. Two fingers dancing in spasmodic twitches, so the fingertips touch each other and make it look as if the boy is writing a message in Morse code.

Randall's own fingers are also twitching and

trembling as he—primarily because he in his confusion doesn't know what else to do—flips to the next page of the manuscript and with a shaky voice begins to read aloud from the first chapter.

Over the edge of the paper, he registers that Chili has stopped in front of his feet. Something about the way she is standing bothers him. At first, he can't put his finger on it, but then it dawns on him.

Chili's gaze is no longer directed at either the nut or the glass jar. It's directed at Billy. And she looks wary.

No. Not wary. Terrified. Scared to death.

Just as this thought goes through his head, the squirrel exhales a shrill hiss, after which it—without letting the boy in the wheelchair out of sight—almost hurls itself sideways and tumbles down the stairs to get away as quickly as possible.

For a moment, Randall feels the same fear and has the same urge to run away—and in that moment, the nagging question he has been trying to drown by keeping it below the surface in the muddy waters of his subconscious is allowed to come up for oxygen.

The question of who—or perhaps rather *what*—it really is they have saved. What it was, they placed in that wheelchair and drove out of the hospital. And whether they should have done it.

For a moment, the doubt is allowed to live in his mind.

But then the boy raises his head and looks at the world around him with a pair of eyes that, for the first time in a very long time, are just as awake and full of wonder as when he saw a bumblebee for the first time.

And then the moment is over.

THE END?

— THANKS TO —

Sarah Jacobsen, my eternal first reader and my accomplice in this life. What a privilege to have someone who not only accepts my need to sit down at the keyboard, but who is also always the first to pull out the chair for me and cheer me on in the background.

Kaare and **Karina Bertelsen Dantoft**, who have been an invaluable team, both as readers and consultants.

Lastly—but by no means least—I owe a huge thank you to you, **dear reader**. Our time is precious, and as always, I thank you for yours. Hopefully, I didn't waste too much of it.

— *Per Jacobsen*